BEARS OF THE ICE

BEARS
OF ICE

THE

The Keepers
of the Keys

Book 3

KATHRYN LASKY

SCHOLASTIC PRESS

All rights reserved. Published by Scholastic Press, an imprint of Scholastic Inc.,
Publishers since 1920. SCHOLASTIC, SCHOLASTIC PRESS, and associated logos are
trademarks and/or registered trademarks of Scholastic Inc.

The publisher does not have any control over and does not assume any
responsibility for author or third-party websites or their content.

No part of this publication may be reproduced, stored in a retrieval system, or
transmitted in any form or by any means, electronic, mechanical, photocopying,
recording, or otherwise, without written permission of the publisher. For information
regarding permission, write to Scholastic Inc., Attention: Permissions Department,
557 Broadway, New York, NY 10012.

This book is a work of fiction. Names, characters, places, and incidents are either
the product of the author's imagination or are used fictitiously, and any
resemblance to actual persons, living or dead, business establishments,
events, or locales is entirely coincidental.

Library of Congress Cataloging-in-Publication Data available

ISBN 978-0-545-83689-0

10 9 8 7 6 5 4 3 2 1   19 20 21 22 23

Printed in the U.S.A.   23

First edition, May 2019

Book design by Baily Crawford

Until they become conscious they will never rebel, and until after they have rebelled they cannot become conscious.

—George Orwell, *1984*

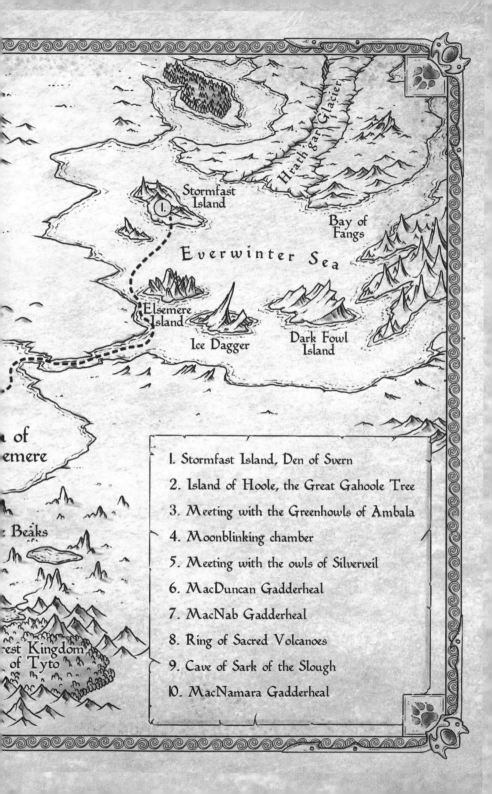

Hrath gar Glacier

Stormfast
Island

Bay of
Fangs

Everwinter Sea

Elsemere
Island

Ice Dagger

Dark Fowl
Island

of
emere

Beaks

est Kingdom
of Tyto

Ga'Hoole!

Prologue

In distant Ambala, in a very tall tree, a dying tree, a tiny spotted owl teetered on the edge of a hollow, crying out into the night. "Maaa . . . maa . . . Mama!" The owl listened for her mother's wing beats. She would recognize them, she was sure. Even though she had hatched out no more than ten days before, when the moon began to dwenk. Rags—for that was what her mum called her—had heard those wing beats signaling that her mum was coming home each night with a worm or a fat Ambala caterpillar or a small snake. She had looked forward to meat. The real meat like her mum ate—a nice plump vole or mouse.

And when that first bit of mouse had arrived, her mum had dumped it unceremoniously, saying, "That should do you," and flown off.

"But, Ma," Rags had called into the darkness. "I'm not sure how to eat meat. What about my first fur-on-meat ceremony?"

Her mother had twisted her head around as only an owl can and replied, "You'll learn on your own just fine. No need for all that nonsense."

The owlet had gasped as her mother, a beautiful owl with luminous spots on her wings, vanished without a good-bye in the gathering gloom of the night.

I am supposed to love the night, Rags thought. *But I don't. Not now!*

All owls loved the night and the coziness of the dark. But there was nothing cozy when an owlet like Rags was left featherless—for her wings had not fledged—cold, and alone.

"Maaaaaaa!" she cried. And then the night swallowed the moon and the darkness began to swallow the owlet and the owlet swallowed nothing.

CHAPTER 1

An Old Spy Reflects

On an island in the far west of the Everwinter Sea, a bear by the name of Svern huddled in his Yinqui den. He pressed the stubble of what used to be his port ear against the peculiar ice. This particular ice was known for its singular properties, which allowed it to transmit sound and coded messages. Thus, Svern, a seasoned Yinqui, the old Krakish word for listener or spy, would know if the cubs—his daughter, Jytte; his son, Stellan; and their two friends Third and Froya—had safely made the passage to Ga'Hoole. And when they did, Blythe, a barn owl and the code cracker, would tap out the news of the cubs' safe arrival. Not on ice, however. For such ice did not exist there. She would tap her message on the roots of the Great Ga'Hoole Tree.

The roots of that immense and legendary tree in which the Guardians of Ga'Hoole dwelled also had the odd attribute of transmitting sound. Svern would wait patiently, but he was not a patient bear when it came to those four cubs who had taught him how to be a father. And he had taught them, or rather advised them, how to penetrate the Den of Forever Frost. That den was where the key to the deadly Ice Clock had lain for centuries. And it was the key that would stop the clock, the source of the Grand Patek's authority. These four cubs had accomplished the unimaginable, and they were now on their way to deliver the key to where it would be safe until the owls of Ga'Hoole could be convinced to launch a flight force to take the key, slip it into the tumblers of the keyhole, and stop the clock once and for all. Those creatures were the only ones who could fly high enough to reach the keyhole. Svern had been cautious, however, when he spoke to the cubs. His mind now flashed back to the somewhat awkward conversation he had had with the cubs, in which he tried to avoid the subject of the possibility of war. *With the key,* he'd told them, *the ultimate control of the clock is ours . . . for centuries no one has ever possessed the key. They did not know where it was, and without it, the Grand Patek's power is nothing but a pretense.*

But then of course Jytte, impulsive and insightful as only Jytte could be, had parried. "But it doesn't seem a pretense. The Grand Patek has complete control of the Ice Cap. He is worshipped by the Timekeepers."

Svern'd tried to ignore his daughter's argument. He'd just wanted the cubs to focus on delivering the key. Let King Soren and the parliament speak of war. *Your sole mission,* he'd thought. *Get the key to the owls. The owls will take care of the rest.* "I must stop calling you cubs. You are nearly full grown now. You are yosses."

"Yosses?' Third had said with more than a hint of disbelief.

"It's not just about size, Third," Svern explained. "It's about experience."

Svern would have liked to go with the cubs on this mission. He knew the owls. He knew the Hoolian ways. But the times were simply too dangerous for him to be abroad. He was too well-known for one thing. His very presence might attract Roguer bears and endanger the cubs. He had to stay hidden. That was how he could most effectively help in the fight against the Timekeepers of the Ice Clock.

Svern had been captured once by Roguer bears and been tortured. They had burned off his ears with hot coals. But in spite of that, he could still hear if he pressed his ear holes close enough to the ice. And he himself was an expert coder like Blythe. He had to keep track of any enemy activity in the region. Therefore, he remained in his den on Stormfast, an island strategically placed to pick up communications from not just the Great Ga'Hoole Tree, but his paw master, Blue Bear, stationed on the Hrath'ghar Glacier, and another Yinqui bear named Long Ice to the north and slightly east on the same glacier. The points of the three dens of these Yinquis formed a triangle that allowed them to pinpoint any enemy movements within that space. It was vital that he remain at his post.

Svern thought back to the moment he saw his daughter triumphantly holding aloft the key as she came out of the Den of

Forever Frost. It was a moment he would never forget. The four cubs had done what no bear had ever done. They had even slain the unslayable, those monsters from the past who had been sleeping for thousands of years and were awakened when the cubs had trespassed the death pits in the den known as the *hyrakiums*.

Svern had taught them how to use ice weapons with which they had killed the hagsfiends and the dragon walruses that had emerged from those pits—and perhaps killed them once and for all. But for the task ahead, he knew different skills would be required. The cubs had to learn the ways of the owls, and they had to convince these owls to stop the clock. Wings—wings were required, but not just wings. The entire kingdom of all the creatures of Ga'Hoole was needed. And this would be hard for the cubs to understand. For the world of Ga'Hoole was a complex one. Much more so than the ice-locked land of the Nunquivik. But they would have to learn quickly, for much depended on the cubs. They were now the Keepers of the Key.

CHAPTER 2

The Keepers

"Oh, and here's one last joke for you! Why did the puffin cross the Ice Narrows?" a strange-looking bird with a chunky orange beak and a very plump body called out from a high cliff as the four cubs swam out of the Ice Narrows. They had been traveling from Svern's den for the better part of a moon against prevailing winds and currents. They had all become used to Svern's company. Jytte in particular had treasured his patience. She always had so many questions—about his own life as a cub; how he met their mum, Svenna; the weapons he had taught them to use. But the one thing she never asked him about was his time in the black orts, the torture chambers of the Roguer bears.

Her brother, Stellan, did not ask nearly as many questions and sometime chastised her for doing so. But Stellan didn't need to ask questions. He was a riddler. He could riddle a creature's mind and often plucked the thoughts right out of them. It was

Stellan who had warned her to never ask their father about the black orts.

"Last joke?" Stellan said in response to the puffin. "I'm sure it's a good one."

"Stellan, don't encourage them!" Jytte growled. Svern had warned the cubs about these somewhat stupid birds and their stupid jokes. They didn't need jokes now. They needed to focus on delivering the key in a pouch that Stellan wore around his neck. That was the only way to stop the clock and rescue their mother.

Jytte felt a wave of pain as she thought of Svenna. Would she even recognize them? How terrible not to be recognized by one's own mum. They were certain now that she was a prisoner at the Ice Clock. But was she still alive? Jytte remembered so vividly that horrible twilight when the Roguer bears had come for Svenna. One on either side of her, with their badges of a prey's blood emblazoned on their chests. The disbelief in their mother's eyes as she was forcefully dragged away. This horrible image filled her head as the cursed puffins cackled on.

The bird had not been discouraged in the least. "The puffin crossed the Ice Narrows to . . . to . . . Oh, I forget the punch line."

"I don't," said another puffin. "Here it is!" A smaller puffin knocked the first one with his bulbous head. The punched puffin went spinning through the air toward the water. The bears stopped swimming and treaded water.

"Great Ursus, I hope it's not hurt," Stellan gasped. The four cubs, Stellan, Jytte, Third, and his sister, Froya, scanned the surface. In another two seconds, the puffin bobbed up. The cubs blinked. Clamped in the puffin's beak were a dozen small fish perfectly lined up. Stellan believed the small, slim fish were called capelin. All the cubs' eyes opened wide in wonder.

"How'd you do that?" Stellan asked.

"Lemme tell you . . ." But of course as soon as the odd bird opened her mouth, the fish fell out.

"Oh, Stellan, look what you made the poor bird do," Froya said.

"Not to worry, madam." The bird dived beneath the water and in a matter of seconds was back with some more.

Another puffin flew down. "Dumpette, you idiot! That's the second time I pulled the punch on you." The bird, who appeared neckless, swiveled his head toward the bears. "Get it? Pulled a punch?"

"Don't speak!" Stellan warned. "Not with your mouth full. You'll lose them again!"

Dumpette—for that appeared to be the creature's name—seemed to be concentrating very hard on swallowing the fish. As she swallowed the last one, she belched. "There it goes. The last one. Number forty."

"Forty?" Froya said. "I thought I only saw ten in your beak."

"Forty's her favorite number," the other puffin said.

"But last week my favorite number was twenty-two. I like twos."

"We like twos!" the friend squawked.

"Oh, Dumpster!" Dumpette giggled.

"Those are your names?" Third inquired. "Dumpette and Dumpster?"

"*The* Dumpster!" said the puffin, and puffed out his chest a bit.

"He thinks it makes him sound more important," Dumpette offered.

"You're brother and sister?"

"Yes, and there are two of us. That's as far as we can count. But that doesn't mean we don't like other numbers." He paused. "I myself have a special fondness for eight."

Jytte's head was spinning. *We have got to get out of here!* "Come on," she said to Stellan, Third, and Froya. "It's time to go."

Ga'Hoole was their destination, or more specifically the island of Hoole, where the Great Ga'Hoole Tree grew. It was from the immense tree that an order of knightly owls would rise each night to perform noble deeds.

They left the puffins, and Stellan felt the pleasant weight of the key pouch made from old sealskin around his neck as they swam on. As they passed out of the Ice Narrows into the sea of Hoolemere, they found the favorable current Svern had told them about, which would carry them to the island of Hoole. But as they grew closer, Stellan's worries mounted. Would the owls even believe that this was the legendary key? Could they imagine that bears as young as they were had actually found their way to the very center of the Den of Forever Frost? Slain the unslayable? He turned to Jytte. "You know, Jytte, I think we should avoid telling them about the hagsfiends and all that."

"Why ever would you say that, Stellan? We did it."

"I mean, they are supposedly very reserved creatures. They might think we're bragging or something."

"Or worse," Third replied ominously.

"Worse?" Jytte turned her head to look at little Third, who could barely keep his own head above the breaking waves as they swam.

"Yes, they might think we're . . . you know . . . making stuff up."

"Lying?" Froya asked. "Why would they think we're lying?"

"Because," Third replied, "grown-up creatures often don't believe youngsters."

Jytte fought down the desperation that seemed to swell within her with each passing second. Not to be believed after everything they had gone through? That was unthinkable. She gritted her back teeth as if she were chomping down on a seal bone for its marrow. *Never!* she thought. She would make them believe.

"We should be able to see the Great Tree soon," Jytte said. She held her head high above the choppy waters and scanned the horizon. "Urskadamus!" she muttered, for a thick fog had suddenly rolled in, smudging the horizon. It was as if the bleak, sunless sky were slamming down upon them, pressing them into a blind world between sky and sea. Not only that, the waves were kicking up higher. Jytte heard Third begin to cough.

"Got a mouthful," Third said, and then began gagging and sputtering.

"Are you all right?" Jytte said. There was no answer. Third was the smallest of them all, and the waves were building.

"Third? THIRD!!! Stellan, I think Third is in trouble," Jytte shouted as the water stirred around her. There was a wild splashing. Without thinking twice she dived under the choppy surface. Reaching out with her paw, she grabbed some fur and dragged up a lump of something.

"Urskadamus! Is he breathing?" Stellan was by her side. Jytte could hardly believe her ears. Her brother never swore but often chastised her for using Great Ursus's name in vain.

"He's breathing. He just up-gutted on me," Jytte replied.

"Sorry about that," Third said in a chipper voice. "I thought there might be something off about that last seal we got before we left." Stellan looked at his sister. Her head and shoulders were drenched in vomit. "Not good to wash down a nice seal spleen with salt water, I guess." The spleen was Third's favorite part of a seal.

"Well, to avoid swallowing more of the Sea of Hoolemere, I suggest that you ride on my shoulders," Jytte offered, then stooped down to let Third climb onto her back.

It was only a few minutes later that they heard a fluttering over their heads. At first, all they could see stuttering through the fog were two large black dots, almost like eyes, that stood out against the thick gray.

"At your service!" a voice rang out quite clearly.

A tiny owl flew out of the dense fog and hovered just above the cresting waves.

"Who are you?" Third asked.

"And what are you doing here?" Jytte tipped her slimy head toward the small bird.

"Function-wise, I am your guide to the Great Tree, Rosie. Named after my great-great-grandma Primrose. Species-wise, I am a pygmy. Ideal for guiding. Please note the two identical spots on the back of my neck. A blessing from Great Glaux to fool attackers or mobbers. Confuses them entirely."

"But—but—" Froya stammered. "How did you know to come find us?"

"Eyes in the sky, I am tempted to say. But actually more like ears in the sky."

"What?"

"Yes, a barn owl picked up your convo."

"Convo?"

"Conversation. Convo is militaryspeak. The Guardians often use shortened forms of words for efficiency. Now, my hearing compared to, say, a barn owl's isn't worth two racdrops. It was a barn owl who picked your chatter up."

"How?" Jytte asked. She wanted to be careful here. This was, in fact, their first ever conversation with an owl. They all needed to act mature and serious.

"Ear slits."

"Not ears?" Stellan asked.

"Not exactly. Barn owls, like the rest of us, have two ear slits. One on each side of their heads. One higher, one lower. But the barn owls' faces curve in a bit, perfect for scooping up sounds. So the barn owl located you, and now you just follow the dots on my neck through this fog, and I'll guide you to the Great Tree. I can fly low and slow, skim just over the tops of these waves." The little pygmy owl Rosie was doing that now while occasionally turning loops and carving the air with her tiny wings. "And you won't lose sight or sound of me. I am noisy compared to most owls. You see, pygmies don't have fringe feathers on their primaries. 'Plummels,' we call them. Most owls have them. They soften the sound of flight. But just follow me. I'll get you there."

"Sorry for up-gutting," Third said. "Hope Jytte's head doesn't stink too much."

"No need to apologize. Owls have almost no sense of smell."

"What?" all the bears said at once. That was unthinkable. They were extremely dependent on smell.

"Just follow me. No time for convo."

They followed the "eyes" in this thick sky that pressed against the tumultuous waters of the Sea of Hoolemere. This was it! Their destination was in reach, and the precious key was in the pouch that Svern had made. They were about to deliver it. And as sure as the stars of the Great Ursus constellation hung in the sky, they had to be believed. For they were the keepers of that key. The survival of this world depended on them.

CHAPTER 3

Blades and Blood

In another sea far from that of Hoolemere, Svenna, the mother of Stellan and Jytte, swam her way through a dangerous maze of gears and hyivqik ice baffles beneath the Ice Clock of the Ublunkyn, the Ice Cap of the Nunquivik. The gears and baffles were the very guts of the clock. They guided the flow of water and were controlled by the escapement wheels and gear trains that transferred the energy of the currents of the sea to power the moving parts of the great clock. These waters were the most dangerous on earth. They swirled with blood from the blue diving seals that the savage bears of the Ice Clock used for adjusting the submerged parts.

On a night like this, a cloudless night, the shine of the stars and the full moon's light penetrated the ice with a terrifying radiance. The sea flashed with the reflected light off the blades of the knifelike baffles and the jagged teeth of the gears. A current began to suck Svenna toward three spinning blades. She stroked harder. But she couldn't escape the suction. It was as if she had swum into a whirlpool—a whirlpool of death. The water was suddenly dark with blood. She stroked with all her might and finally pulled herself out from the sucking current.

In Svenna's mind, it was like swimming through a pod of krag sharks, the most vicious monster in the Nunqua Sea. But at least she was not tethered like the poor seal slaves. And after her near-deadly encounter, she became more proficient in dodging the whirlpools that spun out from the blades and the toothed wheels of the gear trains. She quickly learned how to gauge the odd currents they created. Still, it was a gruesome journey, fraught with the terror of instant death.

She had long suspected a system like this had powered the clock, but she had never expected to be swimming through this lethal maze, and never imagined that it would be her route of escape from the imprisonment she had endured for—well, to be exact—380 days, 9,120 hours, 547,200 minutes, or 32,832,000 seconds. Shocking! Shocking that she could calculate so precisely down to the second, or even millisecond.

Svenna knew that she had to stop thinking this way, but for over a year she had been just that, a calculator! She was smart. The horrible Mystress of the Chimes realized that almost immediately after her capture and had placed her in the Oscillaria, where she had quickly risen to the highest grade. Yes, she had become a fantastic calculator but in the process had forgotten how to be a bear.

But a few moons before, she had begun to seriously explore possible escape routes. In her explorations, she had discovered some secret ice tunnels. On her very last day at the Ice Clock, she made an astonishing discovery. She had followed one tunnel that became a slide wet with seawater. She skidded down it and landed in a shallow pond swirling with blood. There a Nunquivik fox was bent over a dying blue seal, obviously one of the diving blues that tended the gears. His tether had been shredded and his body crisscrossed with dreadful wounds.

The seal's name was Jameson. But nothing could have been more astonishing to Svenna than the moment when the fox, who had been nursing the poor creature, turned around, and there, before Svenna's very eyes, an ancient fanciful tale of shape-shifting creatures became anything but fanciful. It was true. The fox began to swell and then change its shape into that of a bear, and not just any bear but Galilya, the Mystress of the Chimes. Her harsh, arrogant taskmaster was in fact a double agent. The conversation, Galilya's words, came back to Svenna now.

Who are you—really?

A *traitor*, Galilya had said calmly. A *traitor to the clock.*

You, the Mystress of the Chimes, a traitor?

Galilya wanted to stop the clock and the destruction that the Grand Patek had devised for the rest of the bear world. *You see*, she had said, *Jameson and I were trying to stop the clock. Stop it and end this heresy.* Her eyes had narrowed as she threatened, *If you go, I'll set the Roguers on you. I swear!*

In a flash, Svenna's true nature asserted itself, surged through her like a tidal wave. She was a bear. She had only ever been a bear. Svenna rose on her hind legs, charged Galilya, and with her massive paw smacked her squarely in the face. The fox-bear collapsed on the ice shelf by the bloody pond, and Svenna jumped into the water and began swimming her way out of the horrendous clock.

Her bear instincts came back to her quickly. She had always been an excellent swimmer. She had good lungs and could stay underwater for at least a minute and a half. That was considered long. But as she swam, she began to take longer dives. She saw terrible things. Tethered blue seals like Jameson, many badly wounded. Had she the time and the strength, she would have severed their tethers and freed every one of them. But she didn't. A few who looked in relatively good condition she did free. But she was always aware that above the churning gears, there were guard bears on ice bridges supervising the seals. She must at all costs avoid being spotted.

Quickly, she figured out how to use random blocks of hyivqik ice as a kind of camouflage. Pressing them against either side of her head when she came up for air, she hoped that her head looked like simply another chunk of sea ice. The water was becoming calmer, she realized. The roar of the baffles and gears had subsided. She was almost clear of this maze of slicing blades and the spiked wheels of the Ice Clock.

Finally, there was complete stillness. A blessed quiet. The quiet of thick ice and deep water. She was exhausted, for this had been her longest dive—perhaps three minutes. She didn't have another drop of air left within her. She had to surface just as she spotted a shaft of light—silvery light. Moonlight. How could this be? The shaft bore through the ice. A stream of bubbles like stars seemed to guide her. Guide her to air. Fresh air. It was a seal breathing hole.

How many breathing holes had Svenna crouched by for endless hours still-hunting for seals? And how too few hours had she been allowed to teach her cubs the skills for still-hunting? She must get to it. Gasping, she tore through the hole, flinging herself on top of the ice. There were no cubs waiting to be taught the hunting lessons of the ice world, but there were stars. So many stars, and there out in front of the Great Bear constellation were the skipping stars—Jytte and Stellan. Hadn't Jameson told her that he had met her cubs and that they had named themselves after these stars? His words came back to her. *They were well . . . and they have names . . . Jytte and Stellan.*

CHAPTER 4

The Mystress of Nothing!

Galilya was unsure for the first time in a very long time exactly what time it was. How many minutes or hours—or could it be days now—since Svenna had attacked her? In all her life, she had never been attacked by a bear—not when she was a fox, not when she shifted her shape and became a bear. She had seen bears fight in her fox days as she trailed them with her sister, Lago, picking up the scraps from their kills. But she could never have imagined their power. That was something the Ki-hi-ru stories never talked about. They didn't reveal exactly the difference between appearing and actually being a bear. Oh, she had acted the part brilliantly, and yet all along did she suspect, or could she have imagined, that enormous power they possessed? She had even, after her transformation, clung to some of her foxish ways. She preferred to sleep with her head pointed north. Like all foxes, she had what was called the Northing. It helped them hunt. They often described it as a sparkling line in their heads that matched up with a deep line in the earth. The foxes used it as a guide for hunting as well as traveling.

For several days after Svenna had delivered that powerful blow to the fox-bear, Galilya's head rang. Her body felt wrong—all wrong. It was as if the immense weight she carried as a bear could not be supported by her fox legs. Several times in the days that followed, Galilya would look down toward her feet, but there were no spindly legs with dainty padded paws. The legs she stood on were thick—thick as the ice pillars she had seen in the far northern hunting grounds when she followed the bears. They of course were not real pillars or real ice, but an illusion. They were actually light formed when a special kind of ice crystal, one with six sides, settled low on the horizon. And now she herself felt as if she were nothing but an illusion. And though her pelt seemed to her to possess a yellowish cast like that of the bears, she knew that to the bears of the clock, her fur appeared whiter than any they had ever seen. She ran her claws through the fur. This yellowish color made her nauseous to even look at. Perhaps worst of all was the emptiness she felt behind her hips. She had no tail but instead some ridiculous little stump. Without a tail she felt unbalanced. And sleeping as she once had as a fox, curled up with her tail wrapped around herself, cushioning her head, was pure luxury. How many nights since she had lived at this infernal clock she had been tempted to shift herself back to a fox just for a sound night's sleep. But she dared not.

Of course, there were many invisible traits of her fox nature that she had kept. Her hearing for one. She could hear a lemming deep beneath the snow, or the tiniest mouse. Bears, although they heard decently enough, in Galilya's mind were almost deaf by comparison to foxes. So why had she done this? What had driven her? It sickened her to even think of it now. But in fact, she had done it for love. *Love.* How ridiculous was that?

But it had not been love at first exactly. It had simply been the fun of it, of shifting one's shape. A delicious secret that she kept to herself when she first discovered this magic within her own body. She felt special, for not every fox had it. It was hers and hers alone. Though in truth she had been tempted to share the secret with her baby sister, Lago. But Lago was just a kit and she might blab. Then she would get into trouble. It was their mum of course who had told them the Ki-hi-ru stories in the burrow. That's what they were supposedly—just burrow stories to get the kits to sleep so the parents could go out and hunt. But one evening, when her parents thought they were both asleep, she heard her mum and *tod* saying something about Ru blood in their family. That a great-great-great-auntie Kai was rumored to have had it. And that's what got Galilya to experiment, though her name then was simply Illya.

First, she became a tern flying high, then diving steeply in open waters for fish. She covered vast distances. But in fact, terns had to be careful of foxes when they were on the ground, no matter how briefly. Flying wing tip to wing tip with both the slowest and fastest birds from owl to peregrine falcons was thrilling. But in all honesty, there was no keeping up with a falcon. Their speed was as fast as lightning.

Illya herself learned what love was when she first spied Uluk Uluk—a bear who always seemed to travel alone. Never went to the northern hunting grounds. Never went during the Moon of the First Cracks to seek a mate. And yet she was drawn to him. She knew she wanted not to fly above the earth but to be on the earth with him and only him. Uluk Uluk. And she was for a while. Until he discovered her secret.

Galilya groaned in her sleep now and thought, *I am neither fox nor bear. I am the Mystress of Nothing!*

CHAPTER 5

The Great Tree

This is the place! Jytte thought as the cubs approached the island. *We're actually here!* Both Jytte and Stellan had grown up hearing about this place in the den stories their mum had told them. They would soon be meeting the king, Soren, a creature of legend in the cubs' minds. But would he believe them?

All these thoughts streamed through Jytte and her brother's heads as Rosie alighted on a rock and the bears clambered out of the surf onto the beach.

"So where's the Great Tree?" Jytte asked.

"The Great Tree is not called great for nothing. It's everywhere!" Rosie spread her small wings and swept them to each side and up above her head. "The fog is so thick, as it often is this time of year, that it's hard to see. You know it's the Moons of the Copper-Rose Rain. Fog often comes in."

"What kind of rain?" Stellan tipped his head to one side in thought.

"Oh, pardon me. I think in bear country they might call this the Halibut Moon just before the Seal Moon." She sighed. Then, after pausing again, she slowly began to speak, as if in deep reflection. "It must take great patience to wait for those seals to poke their snouts up. Don't you get bored?"

"Never, if you're hungry," Third said.

"Not into delayed gratification myself," Rosie said cheerfully. "From high above, I see a vole skittering about, and holy racdrops, I'm on it like a bolt of lightning cracking from the sky. Bam!" She clapped her wings together, which made no sound at all. But the bears blinked as the tiny owl appeared to double in size as two previously invisible tufts on either side of Rosie's head stood straight up. She noticed that one of the bears gasped.

"Oh, forgive me, I accidentally slipped into threat mode. My tufts. I know—impressive, aren't they? I'm a pygmy, as I said. Southern pygmy owls don't have the tufts. I'm a northern pygmy. The tufts are part of the deal."

Just as Stellan found himself wishing that Rosie would stop with the chatter and get on with it, a much larger owl with a beautiful, white heart-shaped face and large black eyes arrived. The feathers of this owl's wings and body were mottled tawny browns mixed with white.

"Bash is the name," he said by way of introduction. "Feel free to call me Basher." The owl swelled up a bit. "I got the nickname in a small skirmish in my first battle. Swooped in on the enemy and just bashed him out of the sky. No talons. No fire limbs, no battle claws." He began rattling off words and terms that were strange to the bears' ears. "I have a double attachment to the colliering and weather chaws. But I'd lost my coals and my firebrand in this particular battle. Just had to use what I had. My body."

"Enough, Bash!" Rose said and blinked rapidly, then spun her head about in a gesture that seemed to instantly convey her impatience with this somewhat boastful owl.

"Yes! Yes!" Bash shrugged good-naturedly. "I admit it. I do run on a bit. Anyhow, I'm here to deliver a message. Da awaits you in the parliament. Bring them through the roots, I daresay. Might be easier for them than climbing."

"I can climb!" Jytte blurted. "I once climbed straight up a tree on Stormfast to escape a skunk bear." But Bash had already flown off.

"Hush, Jytte!" Stellan reprimanded. Then Stellan turned to Rosie. "He said his da awaits us. Who is his da?"

"Soren."

"Soren the king?"

"Indeed."

"Our da told us that the owls of the Great Ga'hoole Tree are very . . . very . . . What were the words he used?"

"'Traditional' and 'formal,'" Third said.

"Yes." Stellan nodded. "But Bash never even told us his father was the king."

"You have to understand that although Soren is king, and the wisest king this tree has ever had, he wears that title lightly. He is serious about his duty, but he doesn't think that being called a king requires more than just a word, a title, or a name. You'll see when you meet him. He is a rare owl, like no other you've ever met."

"Before we go, I have another question," Stellan said.

"Certainly." The little owl turned toward them and blinked. A shiver ran through Stellan. He was unaccustomed to creatures with such bright yellow eyes.

"How did you know we were coming?"

"Your own da, of course, Svern of Stormfast. He tapped it out in code from his *Yinq*. He's a Yinqui, isn't he?"

"Yes, but that means he listens, he was a spy," Froya said. Her brow crinkled. "But then, of course, he had to tell, communicate what he heard, I suppose. Silly that we wouldn't realize this."

"There's a code. A very ancient code he used. Never been broken."

"But how do you know this code?" Jytte asked.

"Oh, I don't. Blythe does. She's a code cracker. Not only does she crack them, she makes them. Now follow me—as I said, you're expected."

"But where is the tree?" Froya asked, looking up. At just that moment, a stiff breeze stirred the air. They heard a ruffling above their heads. The fog dissolved, as did every cloud. There was only an immense canopy of branches that seemed to stretch across the entire night. And suspended from the branches were glistening threads with ripening berries. "The milkberries are almost ready to harvest. Wait until you taste milkberry tea or milkberry fritters." Svern had told them that the owls of the Great Tree had unusual eating habits and even *cooked* their food.

Jytte felt a soft clunk on the top of her head. "Is this a milk-berry?" she said, picking it out. But it was not the shape of any berry she had ever seen.

"Oh, Great Glaux, no!" Rose giggled. "That's a pellet. You're under a yarping branch."

"A what?" Froya asked.

"A pellet. We have very odd digestive tracts. In fact, we are quite proud of this. All the rest of the animals in the world are wet poopers."

"Wet poopers!" Stellan was stunned. Their mum had always scolded them for poop talk. And their father had said that these owls were reserved creatures, traditional, formal, "with impecca-ble manners," and here this tiny owl Rosie was talking about poop.

"You see," Rosie continued, "we have the ability to compress certain parts of our waste into neat pellets that we then yarp up through our beaks."

"Yeeeecch!" Third said.

"Yes, I know it seems astonishing."

Astonishing, thought Jytte, was not the word she would have chosen. Try "*disgusting,*" she thought.

"We feel that Glaux blessed us with this form of digestion."

"Blessed?" Jytte asked.

"Oh, please don't mistake me. I don't mean to sound superior. I mean, we are all Glaux's creatures."

Glaux, Svern had told them, was the owl equivalent to Great Ursus. There was even a constellation called the Great Glaux.

"This way, please. Enough pellet talk. Follow me."

They walked through a tangle of aboveground roots that were as tall as their shoulders when they stood upright. The ground began to slope down steeply. The bears crouched now.

"Here we go!" Rosie called cheerfully.

Now the path was climbing up through the interior of the massive tree trunk. It was so wide that an occasional owl would swoop by them. The owls were all quite curious about the spectacle of the bears and would often do the most peculiar things with their heads as the bears passed. To catch a better look, they would twist their heads in almost a complete circle, and a few times, an owl, while flying forward, would flip its head back and upside down so its crown brushed the back of its shoulders. The bird would then turn its face completely upside down for a better look.

Jytte, who was in the lead, stopped in her tracks. "Holy Ursus—I mean, Great Glaux . . . how did she do that?"

"Me! Me! You're talking about me." Another tiny owl flew back and began hovering just in front of Jytte, all while flipping its head this way and that.

"That's some trick," Jytte said.

"Not a trick at all. Part of our natural equipment," the owl replied.

"Tink!" Rosie said. "Quit showing off."

"I'm not showing off. We can all do it."

"But how?" Stellan asked.

"You see, an owl's neck is a very odd thing compared at least to other birds'," the owl called Tink explained. "We have extra bones in our necks that allow us to swivel, flip, and twist our heads."

"What kind of an owl are you?"

"Elf owl, smallest of all species and proud of it."

"Don't brag, Tink."

"I'm not bragging, Rosie. It's the truth. A statement of fact."

There was a slight slithering sound as a pink-colored snake slipped over the ledge. She coiled up neatly and began swinging her head. The four cubs froze in horror. Their last encounter with snakes had been with the deadly frost vipers as they made their way through the ice crevasse on Stormfast Island. But Rosie did not seemed frightened in the least. She was greeting the snake warmly.

"Oh, Mrs. Minette, you've been told about our new visitors."

"Yes, I can feel their vibrations. Quite a wake they create."

"Who's that?" Froya whispered.

"I'm right here, dear. No need to whisper. I might be blind, but my hearing is fine. Good as any owl's if you count my unique skills for detecting the most minuscule vibrations. Even vermin. I can track down any bug no matter how small."

"Mrs. Minette is a nest-maid. She tends to our hollows and serves in the dining hall. She is absolute death to any pests, parasites, or other creepy-crawly things that can infest a nest or a hollow."

"And thank you for not saying lowlife. A term we snakes shy away from." She twisted her head toward the bears. Where her eyes would have been there were simply two small dents. "I've prepared hollows for you. Two large galls have been excavated on the southeast side of the tree. Perfect for accommodating yosses."

And with that, Mrs. Minette slithered off. Jytte thought to herself that never in her life had she seen anything like this tree. Her own head was almost spinning, and she wouldn't be at all surprised if it flipped backward and upside down at any second.

CHAPTER 6

A Parliament of Owls

Stellan's eyes moved slowly as he scanned the parliament hollow. Neither he, nor any of the other bears, had ever seen such a sight. First of all, there were candles. Svern had told them about candles, but he hadn't told them about the shadows that could be cast in such a light in an enclosed space. The shadows of all the owls, the members of the parliament who numbered more than a dozen, were cast in the amber glow of the hollow against the walls. The owls sat on a long, curved birch branch. And although they were very still, their shadows seemed to have an antic dance of their own in the flickering candlelight. Stellan knew the names of very few species of owls. His father had once told him that there were more than one hundred. Some very large and some tiny like Rosie and Tink.

"That one must be a great gray," Stellan whispered to Jytte. "They're the biggest, Da said."

There was a barn owl next to the great gray that much resembled Bash. Possibly a sister. On a gnarled branch jutting out from the wall encrusted with lichen and draped in hanging moss was another barn owl. The ancient owl was frail and his eyes were clouded, as old eyes sometimes became. And yet the young bears knew that this was the king. He needed no crown, no throne, no scepter. No battle claws or swords. He was simply majestic and possessed an unnamable power. He appeared luminous in spite of his tattered feathers. He was most essentially Soren, monarch of the Great Tree. Warrior who vanquished the Pure Ones. The most legendary of all the Guardians of Ga'Hoole.

"Come forward, young'uns," he addressed them in a croaking voice.

The bears hesitated, but Stellan's curiosity got the best of him. The eyes of the owl, although dim, drew him forward. He had to see this owl.

"Yes, please come even closer, young'un. My eyes have begun to fail. Neither daylight, nor candlelight"—he tipped his head toward one of the thick candles—"are any longer my friends. But in the pitch of night with no clouds, I can see the stars."

The other bears tentatively took a step or two closer. The king tipped forward at a precarious angle. Jytte held her breath, thinking he might fall, but of course that was stupid. He still had his wings.

"We bring greetings from our father." Stellan nodded his head. The pouch with the key swung a bit as he spoke.

"A good bear, Svern," Soren replied.

"We also bring something else," Jytte offered.

Urskadamus, Stellan almost swore out loud. Jytte was so impulsive. Why had she just blurted that out? They should have waited.

"And what might that be?"

Uh-oh! thought Third. *If Jytte just blurts everything out . . .* Third did not finish the thought.

"Uh . . . I mean the—" Jytte began, but Stellan put a hand on her shoulder to stop her.

She fell silent and Stellan continued for them. "As you know, sir, there is trouble in the Far Ice, the Nunquivik. There is this . . . this . . . monstrous Ice Clock."

"So I have heard, and a brutal leader who thinks he is Glaux— pardon me, Great Ursus. I mean no disrespect." There was a shiver of fear in the king's tone that all four bears found deeply disturbing. "Please continue."

Stellan lightly touched the pouch holding the key with his second claw. He had to do this right in order to convince Soren of how serious the situation was. That they were all imperiled. "The clock—" His voice broke on the word *clock*. *Oh Urskadamus,* he thought. *I sound like a yearling still on his mum's milk!* He began again. "The clock must be stopped." He paused and took a breath. "It must be stopped, because if it isn't, these murderous bears will continue with their false worship of this clock. Every day, young cubs known as Tick Tocks are sacrificed to keep this clock running. The clock has no hunger. That is a lie. The clock is a mechanical thing, but the real hunger is the Grand Patek's for power. The only thing that can stop the clock is the key in this pouch." Stellan lightly tapped the pouch his father had made for the key.

"And so you found it? You penetrated the ice maze and entered the Den of Forever Frost, where the noble Svree once presided at the council of bears in the Ice Star Chamber?"

All four bears nodded. They were holding their breath.

They have to believe us! Froya thought. *What if they don't?* The question clanged in Froya's head as Stellan stepped forward, closing the gap between himself and Soren.

"And what do you want from us?" Soren asked.

"Your help, sir. The help of the owls of this Great Tree. The help of the Guardians of Ga'Hoole."

"Really, now?" The owl seemed to drag the two words out.

"Well, yes, sir," Stellan continued. "I mean . . . uh . . . you know." Jytte's heart was thumping, and a thumping bear heart was louder than that of an owl one, but she was frightened. She didn't like the way Stellan was almost stammering.

"I know what? Please explain," Soren asked. *Urskadamus!* Jytte swore silently. This king was playing her brother. Stellan, in the meantime, could almost riddle his impatient sister's mind. Her frustration was sizzling in his bones. He reached out behind him and touched her lightly with his claws, a warning sign if she were paying attention. *Let me handle this and just shut up, Jytte!* Stellan felt that the owl was not "playing" him. He was sincere. He saw it in those black eyes set in the lovely white face. There was honesty and genuine curiosity in the darkness of those eyes.

Stellan had to convince the king that the help of the Guardians was needed. But did he have to blurt it out? *Because you have wings and we don't?*

"Sir . . ." Stellan was trying to control his voice, which was suddenly quavering. He wasn't sure if he was somewhere between sobbing or shouting out in desperation. "Sir," he began again. "It's because the clock must be stopped. The clock is huge. We cannot fly up there and put the key into the keyhole." He took a deep breath. The candle near Soren seemed to quiver as he sucked in the air. "But you, sir, and these owls"—he turned slightly and swept his head toward the owls perched on the curved branch—"you can! You are Glaux blessed with wings!"

"And just like that"—Soren fluttered his port wing for emphasis—"you expect me to commit owl troops for this endeavor?"

There was silence. Then, to Stellan's regret, his sister spoke up.

"Our father told us about the Frost Beak unit and the medics led by a noble owl called Cleve. And—and others—" she stammered.

Soren looked at each of the bears for what seemed like endless seconds. He turned his head toward those assembled owls, the members of the parliament. He then quickly flicked his head back to the four bears.

"Bears, let me tell you a story. It's a story of the first time I entered this parliament seeking the help of the old monarch Boron, the wonderful snow owl who ruled this tree. I too was with my three dearest friends, Gylfie, Twilight, and Digger, asking for help. And here is what Boron told me: 'The nobility of the owls you see here in the parliament has not simply been given, nor has it been earned through courageous acts. Indeed, nobility is not always found in the flash of battle claws or flying through the embered wakes of firestorms, or even in making strong the weak, mending the broken, vanquishing the proud, or making powerless those who abuse the frail. It is also found in the resolute heart, the gizzard that can withstand the temptations of false dreams, the mind that has the imagination to comprehend another's pain.' That is what he said. No, I don't doubt that you young'uns don't lack in any of those capacities. And I don't doubt that you have been tested in your young lives. I see some scars on you already." His eyes settled on the toothwalker scar that streaked Stellan's haunch. "To have reached the Den of Forever Frost, you must have encountered the 'remnants,' as we call those monsters who have lain sleeping for centuries upon centuries. But it is going to take more than owls to solve this problem. To stop the clock. It is going to take hundreds—no, thousands—of creatures of resolute hearts.

"So what I can offer you is this: I can keep your key secretly tucked away in one of the highest hollows of the tree, but you"— he paused and looked first at Stellan, then shifted his gaze to the other bears—"must first agree to this proposition. All four of you must go out to Ambala, to the Shadow Forest, to Tyto, to Silverveil, and beyond the Beyond. In other words, you must travel to all the regions of the Ga'Hoolian world and bring together an alliance of good creatures—all the good creatures in this world of ours. The clan wolves of the Beyond. The gree-nowls of Ambala. You must understand that to us the Nunquivik is far away. It is hard to imagine this Ice Clock, this cruel bear who demands worship of this false god. It is distant in our minds and in our hearts and gizzards. And to win a creature to your cause, you must first reach its gizzard, or perhaps for species other than owls I must say its heart, or, if they be wolves, its marrow. That is what you need—an alliance, a team of hearts, gizzards, and bone. So go to the lands that stretch from here to the Beyond and gather your team. Then come back and we shall fly with you to the clock. But mind you, it will take more than simply the turn of a key to defeat this monstrous creation."

Stellan almost staggered as the king said these words. The task Soren had just set seemed overwhelming. Bears by nature were lone creatures. The very notion of forming an alliance was completely foreign to them.

More than simply the turn of a key; the words echoed in Stellan's mind and clashed with what their father had told them: that delivering the key was their sole mission. *Get it to them. The owls will take care of the rest.* This alliance would be so much more complicated than just getting the key to the owls. How could they ever achieve what the king was saying? *What do I know about this new country, this land that is iceless? Frostless! The bears that live here are not even white but brown. The wolves live in something called "clans."*

"I know what you must be thinking, young'un. What I just told you about traveling to all these regions—meeting creatures whose natures are mysterious at best to you—seems impossible. But you will learn."

"How, sir, shall we learn?" Third spoke up now for the first time.

"Here. Here at the Great Tree. I am not going to send you out with no preparation. You are going to have to study and study hard. You will learn first more about us here at the tree and those owls and creatures in other territories. You certainly are not foolish enough to think that stopping the clock will put an end to the Grand Patek's and his followers' power."

The bears said nothing, though they were tempted to say, *Why not?* Stellan himself was inclined to say, *Yes, we are that stupid, sir.* But he dared not. However, Third, the smallest, did step forward. "There is something more that must be done, sir?"

Now Soren lofted off his perch and settled directly in front of Third. "Bend down, young'un, so I can see you closer. We can stop the clock." But then he swiveled his head and addressed them all. "Do not doubt in the least that what will follow stopping this infernal clock will be war, and that is what we must prepare for! War! And for that we need more than wings. And Glaux forbid if they find hireclaws, for there are always traitors in any species—hireclaws or hireteeth, outclanner wolves or whatever. So we have to be prepared. We have to be on a war footing." He looked down at Third's tiny paw. "Or a war talon!"

He raised his port leg and raked the air. A huge and fearsome shadow of his menacing talons slashed across the parliament hollow.

Stellan had one thought: *We are in for so much more than we ever imagined.* Had their father known this when he bid them farewell?

The bears were directed to their hollows on the southeast side of the tree. Two immense connecting galls had been hollowed out for them. Dismayed and depressed, they sank down on piles of fluffy down feathers.

Stellan emitted a deep sigh. "Well, that didn't go quite as I expected."

"Quite!" Jytte gave a low snarl of derision. "I would say it didn't go at all."

"No! No, I disagree, Jytte," Third said. "We made some progress. I mean, Soren agreed to keep the key for us while we go out to find allies. That's something."

"After we learn about the creatures of all the regions of Ga'Hoole and everything else there is to know," Jytte said. "I heard that one-eyed spotted owl talking about teaching us special owl words and geography and customs. That just seems like a big waste of time to me. If it's war, we have to learn to fight with weapons. But we already know how to fight. Look at what Froya did with that ice splinter. She killed the hagsfiend with one shot. Right into its skull."

"Calm down, Jytte," Stellan said.

"What do you mean, calm down? We're wasting time here."

"No, we aren't!" Third said forcefully. "Listen to me, Jytte. Did we waste time when we spent all those moons with Skagen before he was killed? We knew nothing about finding our way out of the Nunquivik to the Northern Kingdoms and your father. We studied maps and navigation with him. We even learned about the innards of clocks, the gears, the movement." Stellan's eyes seemed to mist as he thought back on those days spent in the cave of the snow leopard Skagen. Svree's Cave, Skagen had called it. It was a strange place with arcing ice bridges and endless passages. From the cave's ceiling, delicate clock pieces quivered in a windless space among the threads of glowworms that created a permanent twilight. And for this reason, in the cubs' minds it became the Cave of Lost Time.

Third looked at Stellan and then at the cubs. "I think we must do what Soren said. If war is inevitable, then allies are important. And if we are to convince creatures to join us, we must learn about them and the land they live in."

CHAPTER 7

Wings in the Moonlight

The hollows to which the yosses had been directed each had two entryways. One was from inside the trunk, and the other was from outside. They called them ports. The ports allowed an owl to reach a particular hollow from the interior passageways that wound through the trunk itself, or by flying in from the outside. So it was with these two galls. Outside now, they heard a stirring.

"First black," Jytte said.

"Huh?" Froya turned to Jytte.

"It's what they call night here. First black. I think I remember Mum telling us." She paused, and her voice became wistful. "That's when the owls fly off to hunt or do their valiant deeds." There was a distinctly sour note in Jytte's voice when she said the word *valiant*. Mrs. Minette slithered into the hollow.

Balanced perfectly on her back were some rather disgusting-looking items.

"Yes, first black. And they call dawn the thief—the thief of the night. That's when they come home to roost. But it is also called twixt time."

"What are those?" Stellan asked.

"Fried caterpillars—a specialty of the tree. And my associates are delivering some other delicacies—a milkberry sponge, as well as some deliciously roasted sugar gliders. We are well aware that you are mainly meat-eaters. We serve the sugar gliders on a stick. Hooliebobs, we call them."

"Sugar gliders?" Third asked.

"Yes, left over from tweener. They're sort of half squirrel–half mouse, but they glide through the tree like flying squirrels."

Just what I've always longed for, thought Jytte. *A flying rodent with a side of caterpillars. Not exactly an "oh yum" moment!* But she kept her mouth shut.

"What's tweener?" Froya asked.

"Preflight meal. You see, this is tween time. Some call it dusk or twilight. The time between the last drop of sun and the first shadows of evening. Oh, how the owls love the shadows! I, of course, being blind, cannot see them, but I feel them—sliding over me like a cool silken cloak, the cloak of the night." She tipped her head and shivered a bit as if savoring these moments.

"But, young'uns," Mrs. Minette continued briskly, "you should look out your port. It's so beautiful to see the owls take flight into the yonder."

"But you said yourself you're blind and a snake. Maybe you can feel the shadows, but flight? How do you know about flying?"

"How do I know? Well, in fact, I have flown."

"You have?"

"Yes. My great-aunt Mrs. Plithiver was the first blind snake to fly."

"How?" Stellan asked.

"She coiled up and flew on Soren's back. Oh, this was years ago. But we all now occasionally hitch a ride into the yonder."

"I don't understand. Yonder? Yonder what?" Jytte asked, and crouched down closer to Mrs. Minette with her nose almost touching the snake's head.

"Sky is the yonder for all wingless creatures and even blind ones to feel, to simply attempt to know. Of course, there are those creatures who have eyes and still cannot see. Poor things! But for us blind snakes living in the heart of this Great Tree, the yonder calls very strongly. Once we found out about Mrs. Plithiver, we all wanted to go. To fly."

Third tipped his head to one side and regarded this snake. She was very peculiar in so many ways. She seemed to have a deeply philosophical turn of mind.

"I don't fly so much anymore. Lower back problems."

"Lower back? I've never imagined a snake as having a lower back," Stellan said.

"Oh, indeed we do. We have almost three hundred vertebrae. I think my problem is around number two hundred forty-five and two hundred forty-six. At least that's what Cleve says. He's the healer for the tree. So with this problem, it makes it difficult for me to hold a coiled posture in a stiff wind. I like coiling up as opposed to flying flat. Nothing like maintaining a good strong coil and flying into the breeze on a starry night."

The bears were having a difficult time imagining what this nest-maid snake was describing.

"But go, young'uns. Look out the ports of the galls and watch them take flight. There is nothing like it."

So the four of them crowded around the two ports on the southeast side of their gall hollow and blinked at the sight. A slow moon climbed into the deep blue of the night. They watched spellbound as hundreds of wings silvered by the moon's light were printed against the darkening sky.

"Look!" Stellan whispered to his sister. "There's the Great Bear constellation with our skipping stars. Our name stars!"

"But that's the one that they call the Great Glaux." Jytte paused and shook her head. "Maybe it's all just the same, Stellan. We see paws and shoulders. The owls see wings."

"Maybe, Jytte, maybe," Stellan replied sleepily, and yawned. The sky was wingless now. The owls had flown far off. The moon too was slipping down into another world. And then, gradually, the night would become starless as the dawn thief approached, and the breaking sun would smear the horizon with the unspeakable gaudiness of pinks and lavenders and vile oranges—the colors that were anathema to all creatures of the night.

CHAPTER 8

The Yinqui's Nook

The moon was growing slender again. It had been too long since the cubs had left. Svern was nervous, for he had heard no news of their arrival. Not a tap had come through from the roots of the Great Tree. He knew he could depend on Blythe, one of Soren and Pelli's owlets—the three Bs, they were called, Blythe, Bell, and Bash. They each had their talents, but Blythe proved to be an excellent coder and decoder. She could crack any cipher and had invented a few of her own.

The listening nook at the Great Tree, however, did not depend on Forever Frost ice. There were special roots that burrowed deep into the ground beneath the tree that could resonate and had proven excellent for transmitting coded messages. Svern felt that they must have arrived there by now, if Roguers hadn't caught them. But so far, the Roguers of the Nunquivik had not traveled as far south as Ga'Hoole. He had alerted Blythe to inform her immediately of their arrival. So far there was nothing, so he had taken to sleeping in his listening nook, rarely leaving the special ice den that Yinquis used to amplify sounds from far away. It was ideal for listening in and spying on an enemy.

He waited impatiently as hunger gnawed at his stomach, but he did not want to risk leaving in case he missed a coded message from Blythe at the Great Tree telling him that the cubs had arrived safely. Although only two, Stellan and Jytte, were of his blood; the other two, Third and Froya, might as well be. He had grown fonder of these yosses than he ever could have imagined.

But that of course was the strangeness of it all. Male bears were never supposed to care about their offspring. It was regarded as odd, even freakish. It was the females' task to rear the cubs. The fathers most often would never see them again. Never give them a thought. But these four cubs had sought him out. There were never more insistent young bears. They had forced him to notice them, to teach them.

Svern had been in terrible shape when they found him, for he himself had escaped from a black ort ice den, where he had been tortured by Roguer bears. His ears torn off. Starved and beaten. But the cubs had not only found Svern—they'd nursed him and brought him back to a self he had never known—that of a father. Fatherhood! Who could have ever imagined such a thing? Svern had trained the cubs as best he could, and then they had gone into the Den of Forever Frost and done what no bear thought was possible—found the key to the clock.

Now he waited impatiently, reviewing in his head all the codes that Blythe might use. It was Soren's closest friend, Gylfie, who had found the roots with "voices," as she called them. Soren then told Ezylryb, the great sage of the tree, and Ezylryb began to figure out a method for sending messages to the Yinqui bears of the Northern Kingdoms during the tail end of the war with the Pure Ones.

Ezylryb taught Soren, but when the three Bs were hatched, it became immediately apparent that Blythe had a natural gift for coding. By the time she grew up, many of the old codes of the tree had been cracked. The spying system between the owls and the Yinqui bears was left vulnerable. So Blythe began to work on a new system that so far had proven to be unbreakable.

Ezylryb's code had been based on old stories and lore of the owls and the bear kingdoms. But codes based on these well-known old stories had become too simple. Any half-educated creature would know them and would be quite capable of breaking the cipher, as the secret code elements were called. Blythe, however, had discovered a hidden trove of Ezylryb's poetry, and she had begun to use that. And then she even began to compose poems herself. A single word from a poem was selected as the key. Each letter was assigned a number value, and then through a "transposition formula," a message could be tapped out either on the resonant roots of the Great Tree or the ice of a Yinqui's den.

And just at this moment, when Svern was thinking about the cleverness of Blythe's code, he heard something. Tiny clicks penetrating the ice. He caught his breath. Forgot his hunger. It was Blythe's talons! Svern pressed what was left of his mangled ear stubs to the ice and listened. Then, taking his sharpest claw, he started to record the clicks by scratching them into the ice. Quickly, he began to transpose the sequences of clicks into numbers that indicated which letters in the key poem could be grouped into words.

Blythe was using as the key Ezylryb's love poem to his valiant wife, Lil, who was killed in the War of the Ice Talons. He began to count in from the left each letter according to the key he had just transposed:

Lil of my life

Lil of my breath

Lil I shall not sleep

Lil I shall ever weep

"Great Ursus!" He sighed and sank back against the ice wall of the listening den. The code was one of Ezylryb's simplest poems. The repetition of the four identical words all beginning with L meant the four yosses. Then, counting in from the L beginning each line as the key specified for this transmission, one got the word *ILIS*—an old Krakish word for safe. The four cubs had arrived and were safe. And so must the key be safe! Svern breathed an immense sign of relief. If only he could know that his mate, Svenna, was safe as well. He left the listening nook and crawled though the long tunnels of his den to the opening.

The moon was gone. The Great Bear constellation had lumbered off into another night far, far to the west, dragging with it the lovely blackness that the owls treasured. The night had frayed to a dull gray, too dull for any star to shine. Svern squeezed his eyes shut. His world seemed empty. Empty and lonely. He had never felt lonely in his life until those cubs showed up. Why had he never realized what he had until it was almost too late?

CHAPTER 9

Twixt Time

For the better part of an hour, as the night faded, the yosses inside their gall hollows heard the rustlings of the owls returning to the Great Tree. Not long after they had all returned, there was a bit of chatter followed by quiet and then something that the bears had never heard—music, an unearthly music.

"What's that?" Jytte asked.

Mrs. Minette, who had curled up on a ledge on the outside port of their hollow, stuck her head in. "Shush. It's the grass harp." The bears had no idea what a harp was.

But then weaving through the strains of the harp was a shimmering voice. It was as if the stars were singing.

"It's Madame Luella Plonk. She comes from the Plonk family, a long line of singers of the tree. Listen!"

Night is done, gone the moon, gone the stars
From the skies

Fades the black of the night
Comes the morn with rosy light

Fold your wings, go to sleep
Rest your gizzards
May Glaux keep
Safe you'll be for the day

Glaux is nigh

Far away is first black
But it shall seep back
Over field
Over flower
In the twilight hour

We thank thee for our nights
Neath the moon and stars so bright

We are home in our tree
We are owls, we are free!

At the end of the song, Mrs. Minette poked her head in again. "Good light, bears. Sleep well."

Oddly enough, the bears, who were not at all accustomed to sleeping in the day, felt themselves growing sleepy. They were each alone with their thoughts. Jytte was still disappointed that Soren had not immediately pledged the help of the owls of the Great Tree but set what seemed to be an impossible task for them—to journey all through Ga'Hoole and create an allied force.

Stellan, however, was curious about the lessons that Soren said they must learn before setting out. *Chaws*; Stellan reflected on the word. What exactly did it mean? And there was the owl who sang, but who actually made the harp sounds that were not like a voice of any creature? What was a harp exactly?

Froya was entranced by the wondrous tree, which provided a place between sky and earth for a community of owls and these odd snakes. It was almost too marvelous to believe, for from what she heard, the Ice Clock in the Ublunkyn of the Nunquivik was the very opposite of this tree. How could earth have two such places? Was this indeed a kind of Ursulana, a heaven? She yawned—now what was it that the owls called their constellation, the Great Glaux? And their heaven—*glaumora*! Yes, that was it—glaumora.

Meanwhile, Third, a dreamwalker, wandered through a dream where he seemed to be climbing that ladder to Ursulana. Or was he on drafts of starlit air making his way to glaumora? Might he be perched between the shoulder stars of Askryll and

Augden or on the wing tip of the Great Glaux constellation? But then, as Third wandered through his dream, the stars began to shift into another configuration that was smaller than a bear but larger than an owl. What could it be—a fox? A Nunquivik fox. Not much bigger. Was this another heaven?

The bears were not sure how long they had slept, but they began to hear a distinct rustling in the tree. Mrs. Minette suddenly appeared at the portal. "Tweener!" she rasped.

"Oh joy!" Jytte muttered. "More caterpillars."

"The sugar gliders were pretty good," Third said.

"Doubt if you'll find a seal in the tree," Stellan sighed.

Mrs. Minette either didn't hear them or simply ignored their chatter.

"Follow me, bears," Mrs. Minette said crisply. Jytte had to admit that she did love the fact that Mrs. Minette called them bears—not cubs, not even yosses.

"Which way?" Stellan asked.

Mrs. Minette tipped her head, and the two little dents where her eyes should have been bulged a bit. Perhaps this was a blind snake's way of blinking. "That is a very good question. Given your size, the interior route to the dining hollow would be a bit of a tight squeeze. You recall how narrow the passageway was coming up to your hollow. But you bears are good climbers, are you not?"

"Well . . . ," Stellan began hesitantly.

"Yes, we are," Jytte snapped. "Or at least I am. I really kind of . . ." She dipped her head, trying to affect modesty. "Kind of invented it."

"Jytte!" Stellan exploded. "You did not invent climbing!"

Jytte's shoulders slumped. "Not exactly invented it."

"Not exactly!" Stellan said testily. "You were forced to escape a skunk bear!"

"Yes, but I did it!"

"And, Stellan," Third began to say, "you have to admit she did teach us a thing or two about tree climbing. We felt we might need it coming here."

"Thank you, Third." Jytte nodded.

Stellan immediately felt abashed. "Sorry, Jytte." He reached out and patted her shoulder. "That was nasty of me."

Jytte shook her head. "I was stupid."

"Nasty! Stupid!" Mrs. Minette interrupted. "Isn't anyone hungry? Now, stop this chatter and follow me—the outside route." She slithered out of the portal. Her rose-scaled body shimmered in the twilight as she began winding through limbs, all while swiveling her head and giving a constant stream of instructions.

"Take a starboard turn at the next limb, then turn to port. We're going to descend a bit more. A gall portal will appear on the trunk, and you can take a shortcut to the other side of the tree. Just cut through the gall; it's hollow. I'll meet you there."

A short time later, they were entering the dining hall. And it was the most peculiar sight they had ever seen. At least a dozen or more nest-maid snakes were stretched out to their full lengths with perhaps five or more owls on either side of them.

"The snakes are tables?" Stellan said in amazement.

"Indeed! We serve in many ways," Mrs. Minette said proudly.

"B-b-but . . . I think it might be difficult," Jytte stammered.

"Don't give it another thought!" a mellow voice whooped. "Because I have. Hello, dears. We've been expecting you. I'm Otulissa. Spotted owl, or more formally identified as a *Strix occidentalis*." She fluffed herself up a bit and spread her wings, which were perhaps a span almost three or four times her standing height. The sight was quite dazzling, and all four bears blinked madly to take in the spectacle. Her wings and belly were splashed with white spots. Her facial disc was marked with concentric circles except where an eye patch covered one of her eyes, which apparently was missing. A war wound, Mrs. Minette had told them. The entire effect was somewhat dizzying. *Like being caught out on the ice in a midnight blizzard*, Third thought.

"We have made a special table," Otulissa continued, "for our ursine guests."

Ursine guests, thought Jytte. *Fancy!*

"My mate, Cleve, will join. He is the healer here at the Great Tree, and I am a ryb."

"Ryb! Scholar, historian of the tree. My mate is being too modest." Another spotted owl waddled over.

"And former WARRIOR!" Otulissa seemed to double in size before their eyes and spread her wings to an even greater span.

"Otulissa!" Cleve gasped. "A threat display is not necessary, my dear, for them to believe you were a warrior."

"This should prove it, I suppose," Otulissa said, tapping the eye patch with her talon. "Lost my eye in the Battle of the Blue Brigade. Alas!" she sighed. "But follow me to our table."

"I have never . . . ," Jytte gasped.

"Never what?" asked Otulissa.

"Never seen, uh . . ."

"Such an arrangement of snakes," Stellan replied.

All four bears appeared stunned as they looked at the nest-maid snakes stretched out and stacked up, one upon the other lengthwise and side by side providing a platform for eating. At each corner, a single snake was coiled up as a support so that the platform could be raised higher.

"It's a snable. A snake table. The late Mrs. Plithiver invented it," Otulissa offered.

"We're quite flexible." A voice came from the center of the platform. "You see, we can inflate ourselves so that we become fatter, providing more surface area for you to eat from. Do come up. We have some more sugar gliders, as we understand you like them, and milkberry pudding. Quite fortifying. And it's the season of the Copper Rain—best milkberries of the entire year!"

Milkberries, the bears would learn, were the mainstay of the owl diet at the tree, for the tree itself yielded these glistening berries all through the year, but each season's berries had their own special flavor. The Copper Rain season was said to produce the sweetest berries of all.

No sooner had the bears seated themselves at the snable than Otulissa launched into a description of what the bears needed to learn before they set out for other parts of the Hoolian kingdoms.

"The first order of business will be to familiarize yourselves with the chaws of the tree. Chaws are small teams of owls. Each chaw has a special talent. Colliers dive into forest fires to collect coals—coals for the tree's blacksmith, coals for cooking, coals for lighting our candles."

"They dive into forest fires!" Third said. "How do they do that without killing themselves?"

"Very skillfully," Otulissa replied curtly. "Then there is the navigation chaw—all masterful flyers, and they work closely with the search and rescue chaw. The weather interpretation chaw works closely with the colliers. In all, there are seven chaws. You shall also have courses in geography so you can find your way to the various regions of this southern world. There are basically five major areas—Ambala, Tyto, the Shadow Forest, Silverveil, and Beyond the Beyond, where the wolves live. There are some other minor regions as well, and you will learn about them too. Now, how are your reading and writing skills?"

"Terrific!" Jytte replied.

"Passable," Stellan said.

"Well, which is it?" Otulissa asked.

Stellan and Jytte exchanged a glance. Their mum, Svenna, had begun to teach them letters and sounding out words. And then when they had escaped from Taaka and stumbled into the strange town of Winston, where the others had lived, they found signs with peculiar words like WINSTON GAS ALL NIGHT, WINSTON 5&10, and CALL 675-2327 (BEAR).

"Jytte and Stellan taught us," Froya replied, tipping her head toward her brother, Third.

"But we learned from our mum, Svenna," Stellan said.

Cleve's and Otulissa's eyes opened wide. "Aaah, Svenna. Of course!" Otulissa said.

"You know her?" Jytte gulped. *Could this be possible?* She steadied herself and looked into the spotted owl's luminous brown eye.

"No, not personally, but you see, I am, among other things, the tree historian, and I know that your mum, and therefore you, is descended from the noble bear Svenka, who saved Queen Siv during the wars with the hagsfiends for the N'yrthghar!" She lofted herself into the air of the dining hollow, then, flipping her head back, commanded the bears, "Follow me. The lessons will begin in my study immediately, in the hollow of the great sage of the tree. Ezylryb, or Lyze of Kiel, as he was once called!"

Ugh! Jytte thought. What lessons did they really need for war? They had already battled hagsfiends, dragon walruses, and toothwalkers. Stellan had the scar of a toothwalker on his haunch, and she had one from a skunk bear on her face. Wasn't that proof enough that they had been in combat and come out alive? They had had experience—real-life experience. Why did they need to study books and maps?

CHAPTER 10

A Bear with a Plan

Winter had advanced rapidly in the Nunquivik. Svenna had been alternately swimming and walking to put as much distance as possible between herself and the bears of the Ice Clock. But she knew that there were always small bands of Roguers on the lookout for rebel infiltrators from the Northern Kingdoms of Ga'Hoole, and most likely looking for her. Possibly an Issengard unit had been dispatched on a special mission to hunt her down. If they found her, she would be dragged off to a black ice ort and tortured.

She now surfaced again. Inhaling deeply, she realized something was different. It was the air. Gone was the sulfurous smell of the two volcanoes Pupya and Prya. The ashes and fumes of their periodic explosions saturated the region of the Ice Cap, the Ublunkyn. She took another deep sniff. She climbed out of the water onto an ice floe and scanned the sea ahead of her. She knew her swimming days and nights were over. This was the last open water. Traveling would become instantly more perilous, as she would be exposed. She would have to make her way very carefully so as not to be spied. Perhaps she would need to *vat-sapoose*. This was the old Krakish word for traveling on one's belly. It worked beautifully, especially on klarken ice, the very smooth and almost transparent ice. And this was klarken ice that had formed not far from Oddsvall.

The days were growing shorter, the nights longer. It was the end of the Ice Growing Moon and soon it would be the jumble moon. So far, the sealing had been good. She had become fairly skillful at water kills as opposed to still-hunting, where one sat near a breathing hole and waited, often for hours on end. That was simply too dangerous. She had learned how to follow the water track of a seal. She could detect the current of their flippers, and she learned the scent of their urine. She had no idea they urinated so often underwater. But mostly she learned to listen. She began to pick up their sounds. She was amazed how chatty these creatures were beneath the surface of the ice. They emitted a variety of noises, from a *chug, chug, chug* to trills and squeaks. As soon as she picked up a trill or the chug or a squeak, she was on it. The seals, however, had one distinct advantage over her. They could stay underwater for as long as thirty minutes. Thirty minutes, forty seconds, three milliseconds, she once guessed, then chastised herself. *Stop it, Svenna! You are free! You are no longer a slave of the Ice Clock.*

Svenna was now a bear with a plan. And the most important part of that plan was to find her cubs. She had a feeling some moons ago, when some cubs were spotted near the Ice Clock on the ice spines, that they might have been hers. It was perhaps irrational. If these cubs had any sense, they would have fled the region. Certainly no cubs had been captured. Of this she was sure. There would have been talk if they had been. Cubs simply arriving on their own in the region of the Ice Clock was unheard of. Nevertheless, those cubs who were spied had escaped the Roguers, and just maybe they had been her cubs. Jameson, the dying blue seal, had told her he had met her cubs somehow shortly after she had left them with Taaka. He said they had shed their common birth names, First and Second—their birth order—that all cubs were given for one year at least, and now called themselves after the wandering stars Jytte and Stellan.

She had to start her search somewhere now that she had escaped, so logically the first part of her plan was to go back to Taaka's den, where she had left them—good gracious, she thought they would be yosses by now! Since the time she left the cubs with Taaka, Svenna had sensed that there was something slightly odd about this cousin of hers. She could never quite put a claw on what it was. But at the time when the Roguers came for her, what choice did she have?

She had to push on—literally on her belly.

Svenna had made good time, and in her third night, she discovered an open lead, where the ice had not yet formed. Halibut swam through it. They were enormous slow-moving fish that swam along the bottom. The lead was shallow, and it was easy to catch them. She feasted. It made her, of course, think again of the cubs. How those little *chunkins* loved halibut. Chunkins was a word she had made up for them. For indeed, in their first few months, they were like little chunks of ice. Their legs weren't very long, and when they waddled about, it made her laugh. It appeared as if chunks of ice had suddenly been animated. That time had been brief, but it was the rest of the time when she had not seen them growing up that she mourned. It would always be like an open wound for her. The time she had missed with those darling cubs.

It wasn't until she climbed out to eat her second halibut of the day that she realized that in fact she was very close to Taaka's den. But so far, she could not track that elusive life scent that bound a mother to her young. Shouldn't there be some sort of shreds of it, remnants? It could not be completely erased. Or could it? It seemed so wrong that she should live on in a universe where her cubs did not exist. She saw a fox slinking by where the lead ended on the coastline. It was a female. She supposed she could ask. The fox might be Taaka's *hala*. A hala was a fox who had attached itself to a bear, following it and eating the scraps left behind from seal kills. In the moonlight, the shadow of the fox stretched across the white landscape and seemed to beckon her. But Svenna resisted. She didn't want to mess with another bear's hala. It went against bear etiquette, for one thing, and most of all, she felt she had to be very careful in how she approached Taaka. She wanted to conceal her presence until she could confirm that indeed she was very near the den and that it was still occupied by Taaka. She swam farther up the lead. There was a convenient chunk of jumble ice anchored in shallow water that she could hide behind. No bear on land would see her there, and the fox had disappeared. She knew for certain now that this was Taaka's den, even though she had not seen her. Svenna would be patient and wait, however.

The moon was riding high in the sky. It began to slip away, and then the blackness of the night was total except for the stars. She peered up at the skipping stars, Jytte and Stellan. There they were, dancing above the head stars of the Great Bear. *Naughty little stars*, she chuckled to herself—not following as they should behind the heel and knee star for which she and her mate Svern had been named.

She heard a bellow. Definitely a male bear. She peeked around the corner of the huge chunk of jumble ice. The night had faded. The scrap of sun that would rise for only a brief sliver of time, perhaps an hour at most, was beginning to gild the coastline. Two immense shadows were approaching the den.

"Gretschwig!" A greeting was called out. A greeting Svenna had not heard since her time at the Ice Clock.

Svenna opened her eyes wide. She stopped breathing. A rising spear of sunlight illuminated their chests, which were emblazoned with stripes of blood. *Roguers!*

How long had she held her breath? How long had this horror lasted until she could recover her wits? It was as if a blyndspryee, that savage wind that came from afar, had blown through her mind. She had lost consciousness for several seconds. Her heart was now pounding so loud in her chest that her entire body seemed to quake. This was no place for her or any decent bear. She could smell the Roguers from where she crouched. It was the unmistakable smell that they carried with them—the scent of the two volcanoes at the Ice Clock, Pupya and Prya! She would know it anywhere. Now she prayed that her cubs were long gone from this den.

Svenna would wait and watch. She found herself hoping that it was not Taaka's den. But she did not have to wait long to be disabused of this notion. For in less than a minute, Taaka crawled out of the den. Svenna could not hear their conversation, but it was obvious that they knew one another well. However, when the Roguers turned to leave, three words sailed out clearly: "*Patek velklynck*"—*Blessed be our Patek*! Taaka was blessing the Grand Patek! She had left her cubs with this she-bear. A horror filled Svenna.

Svenna had to think. Should she confront Taaka? Could she? If she did, she had to wait until the Roguer bears were far away. If there was any sound of a confrontation, any violence, they would hear it. The ice was growing thicker. The lead was closing up fast. The conditions were becoming perfect for still-hunting. There would be a good chance that Taaka would go out for seal. If the winds were right, Svenna could follow her and meet her not in her den but out on the Far Ice.

CHAPTER 11

The Skylblad's Last Stab

Taaka had been traveling for several hours through the short light, as it was called during the long dark of winter. The wind shifted, and she lifted her muzzle. A new scent alerted her. But was it new or something old and yet strangely familiar? She continued across the ice. She began to have an eerie sensation that someone was following her. But she saw nothing, except it did seem as if a chunk of jumble ice she had passed some time ago was closer. How could that be? The air was so dry. No meltwater, so it couldn't slide on its own. *But supposing it is not on its own?*

Just then a figure came out from behind the jumble ice.

"Hello, Taaka, I'm back for my cubs." Svenna began advancing.

"Wh-wh-what cubs?"

"Mine, Taaka. How quickly you forget."

"Oh, them." There was something in her voice that was like grit in Svenna's heart.

"Yes, them!"

"Svenna, why would you ever think they would still be with me? They must be yosses by now. Out on their own."

"Do you know where?" There was no response. "Would your visitors know where?"

"What visitors?" Taaka managed to ask.

"The two Roguer bears."

Confusion swam in Taaka's dark eyes. It was as if she was weighing her options but sensed time was running out. She lowered her head, emitted a hissing sound from her nostrils, and then charged. Svenna dodged but not enough. Taaka smacked into Svenna, setting her off balance. Before Svenna could think, Taaka was on top of her. She heard the creak of Taaka's jaws opening. The first move in any bear fight was the *krakyaw*. But females seldom fought. Still, she should have known. She felt Taaka's fangs sink into the top of her head. *Better than my neck!* Svenna thought. She shut her eyes. She felt a surge of energy, not pain, run through her. She bunched her shoulders against the enormous weight of Taaka, and curled up. Summoning every muscle, every fiber in her body, she bucked. She felt the weight fall off. Taaka was now sprawled on her back.

Perfect! Svenna thought. With one jump, she could tear open Taaka's exposed chest and rake out her heart! Svenna leaped, but at the same moment, Taaka rolled. She was now staggering to her feet again and in her left paw she held a *skylblad*! This was a weapon carried by the most elite of the Roguer unit. The most dangerous of all weapons of the Ice Cap; it was made of ice, oddly enough forged in the mouth of extinct volcanoes. So this was what Taaka had become—an elite Roguer herself? Or at least in league with the tyranny of the Ice Clock? And this bear was now advancing on her. Taaka was limping and seemed to move crookedly, as if her hindquarters were not aligned. Svenna realized that she must have hurt her in some way. But was it good enough? She knew that skylblads, although deadly, were limited in the number of times they could be used for killing before they became useless. But one stab and the victim was dead. *More than dead*, she had once overheard an Issengard say at the Ice Clock. Where had Taaka tucked it away when she had gone out to still-hunt? How had it just suddenly appeared? There was no time to think.

Svenna crouched down. The two bears had locked their gazes as they moved around each other slowly, growling and gauging each other's strength. Taaka gripped the skylblad in her teeth. The light of the moon glinted off its icy edge. To use it, Taaka would have to stand up. It appeared as if she was on the brink of doing just that. Taaka began to rise. In the next second, she lunged. The two bears rolled as Svenna clawed at her neck. Taaka roared in pain. The skylblad slid across the ice. They both scrambled for it. Their paws grabbed it together. Flat on their bellies, they wrestled with the lethal weapon between them. Then, suddenly, Taaka screeched. She dropped her paw. The knife fell. Svenna seized it and immediately stabbed Taaka. A terrible odor engulfed them. The fur where she had been stabbed seemed to smolder as Taaka's eyes rolled back in her head. Dead. *She's dead*, Svenna thought, and in that same moment, the shadow of a fox slid over the blood-streaked white fur of Taaka.

Svenna looked down at the ice. The skylblad was gone. She looked around. Where had it gone? There was not a trace of it. This must have been its last stab.

"Gone," a voice yipped. "Its last stab. Last murder. Just gone."

It was the voice of a fox. But when Svenna looked around, the fox had vanished.

CHAPTER 12

Lago

Had Illya really gone that far? All the way to the Ice Clock at the Ublunkyn? If she had, was there any chance she would still be alive? Lago had smelled the scent of her sister on that female bear. The one who survived the fight she had just witnessed. There was actually a tangle of scents on that bear in addition to the horrible scent of the dead bear, the one called Taaka. She knew Taaka. She had followed her for several seasons. However, she was a mean bear, so Lago finally had stopped following her. Then it dawned on her. That bear, the one called Svenna, was the mother of the cubs who had been left with Taaka. That was one of the other scents she had picked up in that tangle. She had tried to help the cubs when they had lived with Taaka and she was treating them so brutally. They had even spent a night in Lago's den.

Lago's head whirled. "Too many scents," she muttered. "Too many." There was the noxious scent of the Ice Cap that came from the skylblad, and then strangely the smell of her sister, Illya, on the bear called Svenna. But that made no sense whatsoever. How could a bear carry the scent of a fox—unless of course she was a shape-shifter like in the Ki-hi-ru stories that had so obsessed her and her sister.

Although Lago was hungry, she was too tired to go mousing, and besides it wasn't really mousing territory here—mostly voles, and then there were the disgusting ice borers, ratlike creatures who bored through the ice with their heads. Their meat was revolting. No, Lago decided she would tuck in, rest up, and try to think about what she had just experienced. That bear Svenna—there was no way she was a shape-shifter. She fought like a bear. A fox might be able to change her shape, but could it fight like that?

It had been so long since Illya had left. But she had to admit she had never ceased missing her. It was an unending grief.

Would she ever forget the day Illya vanished?

They would of course talk endlessly about the Ki-hi-ru stories and what it might be like to change into another animal. They would sometimes pretend that they were birds or whales. But it had all seemed like a game. Something that she and her older sister could only talk about when their parents were away hunting.

She remembered those conversations so well. Lago herself was so young that at first she hardly understood when her sister, with a delicious bright light in her eyes, would begin to talk about the shape-shifter stories.

Then it was during Lago's third season out on the ice, during the jumble moon, that they began following an older bear. He was not a chatty fellow at all, as some can be. He seemed rather sad, and Lago could not understand her sister's attraction to him. But Lago came across them once sitting together on a slab of jumble ice with their heads tipped toward the sky that was throbbing with the lights of *ahalikki*. There was a companionable silence between them. Neither one uttered a word, but you felt that there was in some way a deep connection. The following morning, Illya was gone. She had not returned to the den that night.

No one ever saw Illya again. And Lago never saw the bear again. Lago and her family had never even learned the bear's name, but they were always on the lookout for him, as Illya had been so keen on following him, claiming that he gave her the best seal scraps. Once, their mum thought she had spotted him far out on the ice. Lago remembered her mum's fleeting joy. But then they knew it could not be the same bear. He looked younger and happier, and a beautiful she-bear accompanied him.

It was a year or more after that sighting of the two bears that Lago was heading north. It was just before she met her own mate. She had been following some bear tracks. Normally, she would not have dared to go this far north, but there was a scent, a tantalizing scent that she could not identify. She had followed it for several days. She knew one day that she was getting dangerously close to the Ublunkyn, and then it came to her what that scent was. Her sister, Illya! The tracks were those of a bear, but the scent was Illya. She must have trespassed and been caught by the Gilraan, the Timekeepers, and their scent had mingled with Illya's. Lago thought of all that now as that smell revisited her and her grief was reawakened. But that bear Svenna did not have the spirit of Illya within her. Surely if she had, she would have recognized Lago.

Lago had never really understood about the Ice Clock and the Timekeepers or what it meant to keep time. Time just happened. One moon passed into the next—the Halibut Moon dissolved into the Ice Growing Moon, and those into the jumble moon.

The Timekeepers, it seemed, sometimes captured not just bears but other creatures as well—those who trespassed to the edges of The Forbidden, the Ublunkyn. Her sister must have been taken by those immense bears of the Ublunkyn. And although all this had happened so long ago, it was as if a terrible wound had reopened and that Lago was bleeding. Bleeding love for her lost sister.

Soon after Illya had disappeared, Lago had gone on and found a mate, Ito. A good soul he was, and she had grieved when he had been killed. How comforting it would have been to have a sister then. But she had no one. Her parents had died long ago, never knowing what had happened to their oldest daughter. Lago's own kits had been carried off by an owl, her mate murdered by an eagle. She felt that she must be the most solitary creature on earth. But one question always haunted her. Why had Illya run off? What was she searching for? She was an extraordinarily beautiful fox. She could have easily found a mate, though she never seemed that interested. How had she disappeared? Still, why would she just disappear?

Lago crawled out of the den now to look up at the sky. The Great Bear was beginning its climb, and right behind him was the fox constellation—Kn-naru the star fox—just where it should be, picking up the starry scraps left behind by the bear. Kn-naru was dragging her long bushy tail. *So beautiful. Not with that funny curve like mine*, Lago thought. Then she spotted the fire tails! Ah, it was a foxfire moon. On certain nights, when the moon was in a special phase and the air quite clear, it appeared, as if the tail of Kn-naru were spraying sparks that ignited the skies in feathery bursts of silver and gold. It was as beautiful as the ahalikki. Such a moon when it appeared was rare, and the Nunquivik foxes long ago had named it the Shape-Shifter Moon. *Could it have been true?* she wondered. Could her sister be a shape-shifter? And if she had been, would she ever come back, come back . . . *and seek me, her own sister?*

CHAPTER 13

The Lessons Begin

"Great Ursus!" Jytte exclaimed as they crawled into the hollow of Ezylryb. It was a most fantastic hollow, with hundreds of books and maps and odd devices that they had never seen before. There were at least a half dozen subjects that they were expected to learn and demonstrate some competence in, from celestial navigation to coding. They had been told by Mrs. Minette that there would be lessons in geography, history, and the culture of the various regions of the world of Ga'Hoole. Without some sort of mastery of these subjects, it would be impossible for them to forge the alliance that Soren had said must be made. And without the alliance, there would be no key slid into the keyhole of the clock! In short, the owls would not fly, but stay in the tree. The Grand Patek would continue his tyranny and Tick Tocks would be slaughtered on the great spiked escapement wheel of the clock.

"Aah!" said Otulissa, who was waiting for them. "You are intrigued by this array of instruments, I see. Ezylryb led the weather interpretation chaw. Most of his work was accomplished by flying out to track weather fronts, oncoming storms and the like. But in addition, he kept meticulous records of the weather right here in our region. This vine is rigged to an anemometer at the very top of the tree. Fancy name for a wind gauge. And this"—she pointed a talon toward a device hanging on the wall with a clocklike face and a tall transparent column above it with what appeared to be liquid silver—"this is a barometer for measuring atmospheric pressure. When the pressure drops, the silver, which is mercury, falls and we know a storm is coming through. Bell, one of Soren's daughters, is the chief of the weather chaw. But now you're going to meet Blythe, the third of the three Bs. So, to work, bears. And just in time—our dear Blythe!"

Another barn owl entered the hollow. Otulissa continued. "This is Blythe. She is our coder, and decoder for that matter. A kind of owl version of a Yinqui, but we do it rather differently. Nonetheless she has communicated with your father in code, and he now knows of your safe arrival. She will be giving you lessons in coding so that on your journey though the Hoolian kingdoms you can report back to us on your progress."

Otulissa blinked and swiveled her head to take in all the bears. "Meet these yosses, Blythe. This is Jytte standing next to me, then Froya, and next to Froya is Third, her brother, and then Stellan, Jytte's brother."

Blythe's head began to swivel as well during the introduction of the bears. Stellan realized they would have to get used to this, but it always made them a bit dizzy, and when the owls flipped their heads backward, as Blythe was now doing, Stellan thought he might up-gut.

Otulissa pointed a talon toward a shelf of books over which hung a rusted pair of battle claws. "We are in the parlor of the great ryb of the tree Ezylryb. This is where he lived and studied. There are maps, as you can see, and many books. There is the *Sagas of the Northern Kingdoms: The History of the War of the Ice Claws* that we shall dip into. And here are the *Sonnets of the Northern Kingdoms*, which Blythe is familiar with and which became a basis for our coding. And so our studies shall begin. Blythe will start with an explanation for the code procedures for communication. Then you shall proceed with her to the roots and learn the tricks of 'scratch and tap,' as we sometimes refer to it, the method of sending out the coded messages. Then back here for some very basic geography lessons."

Borrrring! Jytte thought. But she saw her brother craning for a better look.

Their instructions began with geography. And this meant maps. They had studied maps previously with both Svern and Skagen.

Otulissa adjusted her eye patch and held the pointer. "You swam out of the Ice Narrows, crossed half the Sea of Hoolemere, and we are here. It is now the season of the Copper Rain, and what might you call this season in the land from where you come?"

Froya raised her hand tentatively. Of all the yosses, she had the least education. "The . . . the Halibut Moon."

"Excellent, my dear. Now, do you know what constellations might be appearing at this time in the lands of Ga'Hoole?"

They all looked at the spotted owl blankly. She waited. Then Otulissa's single eye flashed with a sparkle of delight. "Grank's Anvil!" she announced.

"Grank?" Third asked. "Who's Grank?"

"Grank was from the time of the legends, but he was no fancy of a feverish imagination. Not a make-believe legend, but a real one and the very first collier. Not only did he dive for coals, he invented the forge and forged our first weapons. This is a constellation that never appears as far north as from where you come. You shall see it, though, from beginning of the Copper Rain moons into the moons of the Silver Rain, which I believe in your land are called the Seal Moon.

"So here are your star maps, and as you can see, we have made them on glimmer paper, transparent paper derived from bingle trees. Place it on top of a map and you can see the stars of each season imposed upon the terrestrial map that shows rivers, lakes, and borderlines between the various kingdoms within Ga'Hoole."

"So ingenious!" Froya exclaimed.

"Indeed, and as you learn the new constellations of this land and the land itself, you will become familiar with the different

Hoolian provinces and the inhabitants." Otulissa paused. "We call it the ILS. Integrated Learning Strategy. I myself was the author of this system of learning. You might find it somewhat overwhelming at first, but you'll see how well it works."

The yosses were given land maps and star maps as well as lists of vocabulary words that included special sections of words common in Beyond the Beyond, the province of the wolves and their clans.

When they crawled into their gall hollows that first morning after a night of study, Stellan yawned. "Can anyone remember the wolf word for the high court of the wolf clans?"

Third sighed. "It's Rag something or other."

"Ragnaid," Jytte answered.

"Good for you, Jytte," Froya replied. "Now, can anyone tell me that other star from the time of the legends? It's near Grank's Anvil, and it burns very brightly."

"You mean the sparks that fly off the anvil?"

"Yes, the brightest one."

"That's the Ember of Hoole," Stellan replied. "Hoole was the first king of the Great Tree. The story is in that book she gave us, *True Legends*."

They studied hard each night and well into the morning. Each bear found something that completely engrossed them. For Third, it was the legends of the owls. For Froya, it was the stars, for there were stars in this part of the world that she had never before seen. For Stellan, it was the odd customs and traditions, and for Jytte, it was the history of their wars and the strategies they used. She was particularly drawn to Ezylryb's history of the Ice Talons wars, in which he had first distinguished himself as commander of the Glauxspeed division.

The bears had become accustomed to the strange night-for-day lives that the owls lived, and now it seemed odd not to go to sleep as the sun began to rise. They accustomed themselves to roasted voles and sugar gliders and did not seem to miss the taste of fresh blood. But what they adored most at the tree was the music. They were absolutely enchanted by the beautiful Madame Luella Plonk. Stellan seemed especially mesmerized by her and would often go to harp practice. Otulissa had encouraged the bears to keep diaries about their experience. She promised never to read them but said it would improve their writing and their reading abilities.

"You see, bears, it is such a shame that you never wrote down your stories, your thoughts. You told them aloud, apparently, in ancient times in the Ice Star Chamber, where the Bear Council met. But there was no record. It would have been so easy to carve these stories with your claws into the hyivqik ice."

So one night, when the moon was still up and at the perfect angle for its light to slide into their hollow, Stellan began to write about his passion for music and Madame Luella Plonk.

It is hard for me to believe that I have spent my short life without music. Oh yes, there were tunes that our mum would hum when the lights of the ahalikki lights danced across the sky, but it was nothing like the music of the harp when the nest-maid snakes weave through the strings of grass. These snakes are members of the harp guild. The owls have chaws, but the nest-maid snakes have guilds that are perfectly suited for creatures who are blind. There is a lacemakers' guild, and a weavers' guild, but the harpists' guild is the most sought after. Admission is very difficult.

The snakes' beautiful rosy bodies slipping so effortlessly through the grass strings of the harp is a breathtaking sight. And Madame Luella's voice is as shimmering as any star. Am I drawn to her for just her voice? Or is there something more? Sometimes I wonder if those fox stories of the shape-shifters, the Ki-hi-ru stories, could be true. Madame Plonk is a snowy owl. She is as snowy white as any fox in the Nunquivik. I am yellow by comparison. Dingy! Whenever I am in her presence, I feel even dingier. If those Ki-hi-ru stories are true, maybe I could become an owl. Would Madame Luella Plonk ever want to be a bear?

Stellan blinked as he was writing. Blinked with astonishment. Could he not write such a story himself about a bear who became a snowy owl or a snowy owl who became a bear? How wonderful it would be to become a writer!

He heard a rustling outside the hollow.

"Stellan! What are you doing up at this hour?" It was Mrs. Minette. "It's halfway to noon. I feel the sun on my scales. You should be sleeping. Isn't tonight your big test with Otulissa? Geography, species identification, mapping—all those things you've been learning for the last half of the Copper Rain moons. Goodness, yoss, get your sleep. You do want to pass, don't you?"

"Of course, Mrs. Minette. Yes! I'll get right to sleep."

By the time night fell, the bears were in the hollow of Ezylryb, each bent over unfurled scrolls of parchment with questions.

1. Name the shared borders of the Forest Kingdom of Ambala.
2. In what territory are the green flying snakes most prevalent?
3. What exactly is a gnaw wolf? Please explain in a short paragraph.
4. Name all the wolf clans and their leaders and identify the only one led by a female wolf.
5. Explain the Bone of Shame in the culture of wolves and the contrition rituals.
6. In which Hoolian kingdom do the bears live? Write a short essay comparing them to your own species.
7. What is a hireclaw? What are the indicators that an owl might be one?

The last question was the one that they were all confident in getting right. The answer was NONE! Hireclaws were owls who had no allegiance to any territory. Whoever paid them got their services as killers. They'd fight for any side.

There was another entire section on code and another on useful phrases to know for the various kingdoms. There was also a deportment guide for proper behavior that they would be tested on. The book was called *The Gentle Owl's Guide to Manners and Protocol in the Kingdoms of Ga'Hoole*. There were sections on appropriate postures for greeting certain species of owls, as well as other animals, and tips on food sharing. *When greeting a dear friend after a long time, head flipping is permissible, except perhaps in Ambala. The greenowls of Ambala tend to be quite formal. They are the only owls that even approach the wolves of the Beyond in terms of decorum.*

In terms of mastering code work, or cryptology as it was called, the bears were not expected to be as proficient as Blythe, but they were expected to know the basic poems and sonnets from Ezylryb's anthology and the keys to those codes so they might be able to tap them out on certain roots. They also had learned how to identify trees that might have roots that were conductible, which could send messages tapped out back to Blythe.

Blythe, despite her extreme shyness, was one of the sweetest creatures they'd ever met. She was always assuring them that they would do well. That they should never be discouraged. If she had any criticism, she tried to clamp her beak shut and just give them a little bit more time. It was never "You're wrong."

Otulissa, on the other hand, could be quite abrupt and sometime verged on scolding them outright. "You should know that!" she would scowl. "You wouldn't want to accidentally cross over from the Tyto kingdom into Kuneer—not a place for bears like you! You'll die of thirst. Remember you're bears. You can't fly out like owls if you get there. No ice, just sand."

Now the bears waited while Otulissa and Blythe went over their examination papers.

"What if we flunk?" Froya asked.

"You're not going to flunk, Froya," Third soothed his sister.

"I'm pretty good with geography, but I think I missed some of the questions about borders."

"Froya, quit fretting," Third said. "We all have our strengths, and we all have our weaknesses. No one is perfect."

"How true!" Otulissa said, sweeping into the parlor of the hollow. "Yes, you all have your strengths and your weaknesses." Otulissa churred softly, for that was the owl way of chuckling. "And you all did quite well. But I always feel it's best to speak to a creature's strengths, be it owl, wolf, or bear."

Blythe, who perched beside her, nodded vigorously.

"Jytte, you shall be the coder. You had a perfect score. This seems to fit with your skills as an ice gazer, reading the obscure cracks and bubbles or air trapped in the ice that hint at what might be beneath the surface.

"Stellan, you as well have good language skills. You have mastered all the peculiar wolf expressions. And that will be your task: You, Stellan, shall be—how should I put it?—the diplomat, the *frynmater*, as we call it—the friendmaker. Good with language. A nice sensitivity. You made a perfect score on the test for *The Gentle Owl's Guide to Manners and Protocol*. Quite an accomplishment for a flightless creature!"

Third was growing nervous. What would be left for him to do? Had he no useful talents? Was he too small for anything?

"And, Third, you sense what creatures might say before it's said, or what creatures might do before they do it. You are a tracker of sorts, not just of minds, but of land. Not just of earth, but dare I suggest that you have all the makings of a dreamwalker?"

Third gasped at this. How did she know? The same thought coursed through all the yosses' minds. "However did you . . . ," Third began, but was so completely amazed he could not complete the question.

"My dear cubs," Otulissa addressed all of them now as she swiveled her head. "When you have lived as long as I have, for indeed I am a very old owl, you begin to sense things about creatures. Perhaps most particularly if you have lost something, as I have." And with this, Otulissa tapped her eye patch with a front talon. "You gain other abilities. There are compensations of sorts." She took a deep breath. "To find the old forge of the blacksmith Bubo, you did it, Third. None of us could figure out how you did it so quickly."

"The coals, ma'am."

"But the coal had long vanished."

"Their dust, the coal dust, was in the ground. I could almost see it the way Jytte can see the smallest crack in ice or a trapped bubble."

"And that is precisely why you will be the tracker, the navigator. You can see the dust of dreams or the dust of coals."

What about me? Froya thought, and Otulissa then turned abruptly to her. "And, Froya, your skills with celestial navigation are extraordinary. You are the only one who missed not a single question about navigating with the star coordinates. You have learned every star's position at any time during any moon. Is that not an accomplishment?"

"I guess so," Froya said softly.

"I know so. Your brother might be a dreamwalker, but you keep the stars safely tucked in your brain, be it night or day. You are a starwalker! Together with your brother, Third, you will make a powerful navigation team." She took another deep breath. "Now that your course of studies is completed at our Great Tree, you shall, with your talents, I am certain, be able to gather an allied force to fight these loathsome timekeepers of the Ice Clock. So tomorrow you shall leave at twixt time."

"Dawn!" all four bears said at once.

At last! thought Jytte.

But are we truly ready? thought Stellan. He knew Jytte couldn't wait to leave. But how could she be so confident? Could they gather this force? Stellan wondered. Would anyone listen to them?

They had not expected such an abrupt departure.

"Why twixt time?" Stellan asked. "We've just become used to sleeping in the day and waking and studying at night—like owls."

"Exactly! No one you accidentally encounter, for it could be a hireclaw, must suspect that you have been with us. You must learn to eat your food raw again. You must avoid phrases like 'Great Glaux' or the curse 'racdrops.'"

Jytte blinked. She had become rather fond of that curse, which meant the droppings of a raccoon. It was much better than the bear version, *gort skrat*, which meant scat of a land creature and not one of ice.

Otulissa then took a deep breath. "Now listen to me, yosses. Together, you are a team, but individually, you are each a chaw, a chaw of one! Congratulations."

Before the Beyond

CHAPTER 14

"My Own Kind"

Deep in Ambala, a tiny owl whined at a rabbit who sat on its haunches regarding her. "Don't whinge, Rags!" the rabbit snapped.

"I wasn't whinging—I was whining."

"Same thing. And this is not a discussion about words. It's about flying."

"But you said that if I just perched on that log and flapped a bit—a bit you said, no more—I would lift off. And now I've fallen. Fallen smack on my butt. Why didn't you tell me it was this hard?" Rags was racked with despair.

"For Lapin's sake! I'm not an owl. I'm not even a bird. I'm a rabbit! I was just trying to give you some tips, having lived in this forest a long time and seen the owls of Ambala flying here and there."

"Who's Lapin again?"

"The Big Rabbit in the sky. Rather like your Glaux." Rags made a sound halfway between a squeak and a moan as she tried to groom her own wings from the bits of pine needles and dirt. She must be the filthiest owlet alive. All because she couldn't fly. It had been almost a moon since her mum had left, and then a few nights later, she had fallen from the hollow. By now, she realized that her mum was never going to return. But knowing and understanding were two different things. "Why, Rabbit, why would she do this?" The rabbit had never divulged his own name. So Rags had to be content with simply calling him Rabbit.

"Why what?" His pink-rimmed eyes blinked.

"Why didn't Mum ever come back?"

The rabbit sighed. He had a sense, a wispy inkling why Rags's mum had not returned. He had seen it in the spiderweb that was strung between the fork in a fallen branch near his rabbit hole. "Glimmerings" he called them, and that was how these notions, intuitions came to him. He was a web reader. He came from a long line of web readers. They were known as mystic rabbits because of their odd gifts. Gifts that were slightly incomplete, and that was the problem. What these rabbits saw in a web was always incomplete and not the entire picture. They could see things that might have happened or might soon happen, but the story was often confused. They never saw the whole picture or story. There was a crescent shape of white fur on the rabbit's forehead that marked him as a web reader.

What the rabbit had seen before Rags had even hatched out was that her mum hardly cared about her. Indeed, she would go off and leave the egg for long periods of time—on cold nights! If he could have climbed up there to keep the egg warm, the rabbit would have. Thank Lapin there was a very nice family of sugar gliders who lived nearby, and he had convinced them to scramble up the tree and cover the egg when the mum was away. Edith was the mother's name—a spiky name if there ever was one! Seemed to fit her. All the thanks those sugar gliders got was that Edith ate one of them. She was a dreadful owl. And she didn't care a whit for her child. And then, one night shortly after Rags had hatched, she was off! It was not exactly a surprise to the rabbit. He'd seen something in the web of that orb-weaver spider that alarmed him more than even Edith's desertion of her owlet.

He had stared for a long time at the glittering web. In the corner of the web on that particular night, he saw an odd tangle. Lines crossing in peculiar ways, as if the spider itself was confused. The web was at first glance rather classic—a circle with radiating threads of silk forming concentric circles within the perimeter. The final spiral at the center, with the sticky capture silk, was crossed with a line from one of the radial threads. Very confusing. What did it mean? That web was gone, but now the rabbit noticed that the orb weaver had just finished another web. It was a bit higher up. He jumped. Almost saw it but not quite. He jumped two more times.

"See, it's hard," Rags whined.

"What?"

"Trying to fly."

"I'm not trying to fly." The rabbit shook his head in disgust. "I'm trying to read this new web. Now get over here and help me."

"How?"

"I'm going to crouch down. You walk up my back, starting at my tail, and get on top of my head. Then describe what you see in this web."

Rags blinked. "No flying?"

"Right. Just walk up my back to the top of my head."

"I won't be too heavy?"

"No!" the rabbit said in exasperation. "You have hollow bones, remember?"

"Oh yeah."

Rags hopped on the rabbit's back and was soon standing on top of his head.

"Now what do you see?"

"Well, it's very large, and it's sort of flat. Flatter than the old one you showed me."

"And the radials?"

"What are radials?"

"The threads that spread out from the middle."

"Oh, those—they look kind of fuzzy. Like they maybe have rabbit fur on them."

The rabbit's pink-rimmed eyes grew huge. "Really!"

"Yes, what does that mean?"

"It means something big is coming our way. Really BIG!"

"Up! Up! We have to get up," Third called out. "Twixt time. Remember what Otulissa said. We can't do anything that makes any creature think we've spent time with owls."

"But there are plenty of animals who are night creatures," Jytte protested. "The ones they call raccoons. Rosie told me that. Badgers, bats."

"Listen to me. We must do exactly what Otulissa told us. We have not spent almost a moon learning the ways of owls, the customs of this new land, to immediately break some of the most important rules they taught us. Remember, our goal is to find allies. Without an allied force, we fail. The clock is not stopped and . . ."

Jytte felt a wash of shame run through her. How had she been so completely distracted from their purpose? And she was the one most anxious to leave. If she had to spend one more night studying star charts without actually being outside under the stars and moving toward Ambala, their first destination, she thought she would expire. Studying was not her favorite occupation. One could spend a lifetime studying and then doing nothing. She was not, nor ever would be, a student. *All action, that's me!* she had said once to Otulissa, who had replied calmly, *Action without study can only amount to a senseless reaction. And you seem to be doing quite well with those codes. So study on.*

Third blinked into the rising sun. It was a new day. A golden pink was beginning to seep over the horizon. "That's east," he said softly. He put on a pouch with the map that he would carry as the navigator. Froya would also carry one. The sun would be to their backs for the first part of their journey, as they would cross the sea south and head slightly west to Ambala, where the greenowls lived. Then, after Ambala, they would begin to angle due north toward Silverveil and eventually cross over into the Beyond, where they would meet the wolf clans. Such was their course with the intention of gathering an allied force.

The tree at this hour of the dawn was at its most quiet, for all the owls were sound asleep as they left and began to swim away from the island of Hoole, toward the distant shoreline. It felt odd to Froya to be getting up at this hour. The morning star, the one called Joss, named for a renowned scout and messenger, was dissolving into the thin light of this new day. *No stars to guide me now*, thought Froya, *just the land itself.* But those maps were emblazoned in her mind. She never would have dreamed she had a mind for such things. But it wasn't just the owls of Ga'Hoole who had taught her. It was the yosses. Her life had seemed so meaningless until she had found her brother Third again, and Stellan and Jytte—and Svern! How could she ever forget Svern!

It was not a long swim. The dawn was still lingering when they climbed onto the beach where the river flowed into the sea. They kept to the west banks of that river. They needed to follow it to the headwaters and then turn due west. Winter was slow to come here in comparison to the Nunquivik. Nothing was completely frozen yet, and there were plenty of fish in the river and they had been told there were otters as well.

Froya stood up and surveyed the landscape. "So this is what they call winter here. The stream flows, hardly any snow on the ground."

Froya squinted at the same map with star coordinates that she had pulled from a pouch around her neck. "There will be even less snow once we get to something called the Brad." She looked harder at the map. "I don't quite understand what this Brad is," she murmured.

"They kept talking about greenowls. It's hard to imagine owls with green feathers," Stellan said, not really answering. "But that's our first stop. Supposedly, they have an alliance with some powerful snakes that have been allies in the past during owl wars." The last really powerful snakes they had encountered were not nest-maid snakes of the Great Tree but the the terrifying frost vipers on Stormfast Island. They had not left Stellan or any of the bears especially inclined toward reptiles. But here he was the designated frynmater, the diplomat. So it would not do to offend the greenowls' friends.

"I'm not sure about the greenfeathers," Jytte said. "But they are supposed to be very smart owls. Well, no sense waiting around. Let's go."

They headed off. The farther inland they went, the less snow they found. How peculiar to be in this place with no white.

There were all sorts of hues of colors. There were trees with still deeply green leaves, yet some had leaves that were very pale green—the same greens as those of the ahalikki that danced in the sky during the Seal Moon. Several trees had begun to turn brilliant colors—orange, bright yellow, and bloodred. And yes, some copper—a color almost gold but not quite. This was an ever-changing land that yielded up jewels brighter than any ice or snow.

And there was mud, some almost black, some reddish. Froya thought that it was as if a rainbow had come down from the sky and spilled its colors across the land. Could she ever go back to that colorless place from which she had come—the Nunquivik? Where a cub must wait until the ahalikki painted the night skies of the winter moons to see such bright colors splash the vastness of Ursulana? Here one did not have to wait for night or winter. Here there were colors in every moon.

They stopped frequently, as they grew tired more easily and were unaccustomed to this new schedule of waking during the day in a world vastly different from the Nunquivik. That world now seemed as distant as any star.

They had entered a wooded area. Jytte was in the lead. Froya was reflecting on these differences as she followed the three bears ahead of her. She looked about, noting every tree and fallen log. It was all so strange. So unfamiliar but not frightening. In fact, it was seemingly benign in a certain way. She then stopped short. Off to one side, there was a very peculiar sight, not just a sight but a spectacle. A rabbit stood completely still, as if it might have been frozen, for not a whisker moved. However, on the very top of its head, an owlet perched. A spotted owlet.

"What?" Froya exclaimed. The other three bears stopped suddenly and looked at her. The owlet gave a shriek and fell from the rabbit's head.

"What? What is it?" Stellan said in a taut voice.

"I cannot believe you just walked by that. An owl perched on top of a rabbit's head!" Froya exclaimed.

"Believe it," the rabbit replied, and turned toward the bears. By now, the owlet was giving whiny hoots.

"Believe it!" the rabbit repeated. "I told you something big was coming," he said, turning to Rags, who was by this time on the ground. "Just get up. You're not hurt."

"Yeah, but . . ."

"But nothing. Wave your port wing." The owlet did so. "Wave your starboard wing." Again Rags did as she was told. "Now wave both." The owlet did and lofted into the air.

"You did it. You did it! Now keep pumping those wings!" The bears were watching this spectacle in absolute amazement.

"I did it! I did it!" Then the owlet's wings seemed to lock above her head in a V shape.

"Pump!" screeched the rabbit, but it was too late. The owlet fell to the ground.

There was a stunned silence. "Am I dead?"

"Not if you can ask the question," Third replied.

The rabbit now leaned over the owlet. "I told you something big was coming."

Rags staggered to her feet and blinked at the bears.

Froya came forward. "What exactly is going on here?"

Rags stepped forward. "I flew. I flew for the first time in my life."

"And you were taking off from this rabbit's head," Froya added in an incredulous voice.

"Oh, no, when I was up there, I was just helping read a spider's web."

"Yes, of course," Jytte scoffed. "A common sight, I suppose." There was more than a tinge of sarcasm in her voice.

"It's a long story," the rabbit said uneasily.

"I would think so," Jytte said. *A rabbit teaching a young owl how to fly. How does that happen?* There were so many mysteries in this new world with all these new creatures. It was a bit overwhelming. Would they be required to ask rabbits to join this allied force? Jytte wondered.

And so the four bears sat down on their haunches and listened to the rabbit. They heard how Rag's mother had vanished.

Vanished, thought Stellan. *Ours did too.* He tried not to think of Svenna too much. But how can one banish such a thought? He could almost smell her milk now—though he was far beyond being a nursing cub. While the rabbit spoke, Rags was so taken with the idea that she had almost flown that she politely asked if she might crawl up on top of any of the bears' heads and practice taking off.

"Of course, be my guest," Stellan replied quickly. The other three bears looked at him in confusion. "It's all part of my job, you know. I'm the diplomat," Stellan said softly.

By the time the rabbit finished the story, Rags, exhausted from her short flights, curled up in a little moss nest the rabbit had made for her. Then the rabbit, looking to make sure the owlet was asleep, turned to the four bears.

"Rags's mum abandoned her, I'm sure. I think her mum is a slipgizzle."

"Spy!" Stellan said in alarm. And just moments ago, he was feeling so profoundly sorry for this owlet. Perhaps the mother was mean like Taaka!

"That or a hireclaw." All four bears gasped. The rabbit nodded. "You must go to the Brad. That is where the smartest owls are. You must tell them."

"That was where we were heading," Jytte replied. "They will be very interested in this."

"Absolutely!" Stellan said. "If there are spies in Ambala already, this will be invaluable information and I daresay will help our mission. We need allies, and if the enemy has infiltrated . . ." Stellan's voice dwindled as he imagined these woods thick with spies. He turned abruptly to Froya. "Froya, get out the map."

Froya took the map of Ambala from the pouch and spread it on the ground. They gathered in a circle and pored over it.

Froya began to explain, "You take a turn there . . . follow a creek. Then you begin to go down a long slope into a mossy dell."

"I want to go!" It was Rags.

"With us?" Jytte asked. This was not exactly the ally they were looking for. An owlet barely out of the shell who hardly knew how to fly. Stellan himself was having the same thought. But he could tell that Third and Froya thought differently. It was easy for him to riddle Third's mind. *She needs a friend. She wants to believe that not all owls are horrid like her mum . . . or like Taaka, our mum.*

The owlet swiveled her head toward the rabbit. "I heard everything. I heard how my mum abandoned me. How she might be something bad . . . something you call a hireclaw or a slip whatever. I want to be with my own kind. The kind that are good. That are smart." Rags's deep brown eyes began to glitter with tears. "Oh, Rabbit, I didn't mean to hurt your feelings. And you are good and kind and ever so smart, but to be with owls— owls who are . . ." Her voice grew whispery. "With the owls in the Brad. I think I knew Mum would never be back. But when I fell out of the hollow, you saved me. You brought me fat worms and caterpillars and even chased a vole for me. You made this nest of moss for me here on the ground. But I need to be in the trees. I need to fly through the night. I think I can now. I need to be with my own kind." He paused. "They cannot all be like my mum."

"No, never!" Jytte suddenly said. She felt for this owlet. She was shocked that she had ever considered her a possible burden. Well, she might be a slight burden, but it would be worse not to help her find her own kind.

CHAPTER 15

"I Am Who I Am"

Galilya, dripping in her jeweled finery, sat stiffly on the ice bench
in the Stellata Chamber between the Mystress of the Hands
and Torsen, the new Chronos. Unfortunately, Torsen seemed
attracted to her. But so far, she had successfully ignored his
attentions. The Gilraan, the elite ministry of the Ice Clock, had
gathered at the summons of the Grand Patek. It was an emergency meeting to hear alarming news. Normally meetings were
called to discuss the reports of infiltrators from the Ga'Hoolian
kingdoms. But this summons suggested a new level of urgency.

The Grand Patek called the meeting to order. "We gather
here this evening to hear a disturbing report from the Southern
Kingdoms of Ga'Hoole." The Grand Patek stood up from the
elaborately ice carved throne that had been incised with the
numerals of the clock's face as well as many of the internal parts
of the clock—escapement wheels, balance wheels, pendulum

weights—all the elements of the mechanical, or moving parts, of a clock. He began to step down from the throne's pedestal—always a bad sign—and within seconds, he began ranting. "Those owls of Ga'Hoole. I have a special plan for them. No! Of course not I, but the clock has a special plan for them. It will constitute their annihilation and our redemption come the day!"

Come the day . . . the three words echoed through the Stellata Chamber. *No*, Galilya thought. *That day cannot come.* And that was why she had to stay. She had to slow the clock, if not stop it. The bungvik could not break.

"They are inferior creatures," the Grand Patek continued. "You know their bones are hollow, and so are their heads!" he roared, and the Stellata Chamber seemed to shake. "Yes, they are pitifully stupid. Except for a very few. I trust that it is one of the few who is waiting to pay respects and brings some vital information." He looked at Torsen, the Chronos, who nodded. "The world of Ga'Hoole has infected the bears of the Northern Kingdoms. Those bears are as witless as the owls. But that world will soon be ours, and those creatures—the leftovers who do not die—shall be contained. They shall not contaminate the world of the clock. But we can make use of such remnants." He paused and seemed to consider for a few seconds. "You of course know if it weren't for me there would be no clock . . . The bears of Ga'Hoole think that Svree invented the clock . . . No. They give Svree the credit. But I am the one who awakened our god clock and set its still heart to beating. They talk about the Bear Council in the Den of Forever Frost. But it's simply not so!"

Lies, lies, lies, Galilya thought. The Grand Patek had moon blinked these bears with lies for years. *Moon blinked* was an expression she had learned from her parents. It came from the owl world and was a condition that befell owls if they if they accidentally fell asleep during the night under the full shine of a moon. Well, the Grand Patek thought of himself as the moon and the sun of this evil world at the top of the Ice Cap. And bears, bears of the Gilraan, were nodding in agreement, for they had indeed been completely moon blinked. She had to get out of this place. She was still unsure how long it had been since Svenna had left after smacking her in the face. Galilya had actually for the first time lost her grip on time. Her grasp of time perhaps, but not words. The last words that she remembered Svenna saying when Galilya begged her to stay were *I am what I am.*

And I, thought Galilya, *no longer know who I am.* The worst thing she had ever done was to listen to those Ki-hi-ru stories, to become a bear when she truly once had been a fox. Not simply *once upon a time* in the way that stories often began, but once in her real life she had been a fox. She realized now that a life had died inside her while she went on living. But was this living? Yes, she breathed. Her heart pumped as it did in all living creatures. But in truth she felt as mechanical as the Ice Clock that they foolishly worshipped.

Eventually, the Grand Patek realized that he had veered from the original purpose of the meeting: the urgent news from the enemy regions of Ga'Hoole. He resumed his seat on the ice throne and nodded to Mystress of the Hands.

"Please escort our guest into the Stellata." The Mystress of the Hands, who sat next to Galilya, rose and exited. When she returned, an owl swooped into the chamber and settled on a small ice platform in front of the Grand Patek.

"Kindly state your name, species, and business."

"My name is Edith. I am a spotted owl, formally identified as a *Strix occidentalis*. I am from the Ga'Hoolian kingdom state of Ambala. And I serve as a slipgizzle."

The Grand Patek narrowed his eyes. "A slipgizzle, I recall, is an owl word for spy. In short, a feathered Yinqui but not quite the listening skills."

"I beg to differ." Edith swiveled her head around to address the entire gathering. This caused a gasp among the bears. "Yes, your shock is noted. The extra bones in my neck provide me with the ability to listen from many different angles." She then, in less then a quarter of a minute, flipped her head and twisted it, ending with her grand finale of upending it so her face appeared upside down facing backward. The bears of the chamber were almost reeling in dizziness.

"You've proven your point," the Grand Patek said. "Now what news do you bring us?"

"The key to the Ice Clock has been found."

It was as if the air had been sucked out of the room. Most of the bears had only the vaguest notion of what the word *key* even meant. However, they knew it was entwined with the legends of Svree. It was their own leader, the Grand Patek, who had breathed life into the clock, making it divine. There had been an expression that through the ages had come down that the worshippers of the clock sometimes muttered when they were having problems with calculations: "Oh, give me the breath of Svree!" But uttering such an expression was now *vorkiche*, or forbidden.

"This . . . this . . . can't be . . . ," the Grand Patek stammered. "The key in the wrong paws or wrong talons is a desecration. It could be stopped. The divine, our destiny could be shattered."

Torsen, the Chronos, stood up. "Are you saying the Den of Forever Frost has been penetrated?"

"Indeed, sir." Edith nodded, her brown-black eyes glowing with a peculiar kind of pride for being the messenger of these alarming tidings. This could only increase her stature among the *zayle vertray*, the faithless betrayers of Hoole. She was a slipgizzle of the third order but surely this would warrant an advancement, at least to the second order. Dare she dream of a first-order advancement?

Torsen now stood up from the bench and went over to the owl. He peered down at her. She was a medium-size owl, with a very round head and no ear tufts.

"You are certain of this?" he asked.

"Of course I'm certain. On my gizzard I swear."

"Your gizzard?"

Galilya clamped her eyes shut. *These bears know nothing if they don't know about the gizzards of owls!*

"The gizzard is a vital organ in owls. To swear upon it is a solemn oath," Edith said.

Ah! The false earnestness of a spy! Galilya thought.

"All right, all right," Torsen said impatiently. "Now who exactly wrested this key from the Den of Forever Frost?"

"It is my understanding that it was four young bears just beyond cubhood."

"Yosses, we call them," Torsen replied.

"And do you know where they took the key?" the Grand Patek asked, baring his fangs. His eyes became mere slits. Dark slits in the whiteness of his fur. It was as if the reek of evil rolled off him. *Am I the only one who can smell it?* Galilya thought.

"Not sure where it was taken. But possibly the Great Ga'Hoole Tree."

The Chronos and the Grand Patek exchanged glances. A silent conversation seemed to transpire between them. Edith looked from one to the other. The Grand Patek rose. He was trembling with anger. It was impossible for the Grand Patek to imagine that this had happened. "These are the keys to our kingdom. To our Clock Divine. No creature can hold these but I—the Grand Patek. I do hereby order *bwatig* on these cubs, these yosses."

Galilya was stunned. Issuing a bwatig, an arrest-and-torture-until-death order, in the Ga'Hoolian kingdoms would certainly be the start of war!

"Torsen, can you gather a force to hunt these bears down?" he asked.

Torsen nodded. The Grand Patek continued in a deadly voice. "They must be brought to a black ice ort and subjected to the most advanced techniques."

Edith interjected, "Certainly, sir. I can help assemble a commando force of owls."

"We have undercover Roguers already inserted in the enemy territory who can undoubtedly help you. Torsen will tell you where and how you might find them."

"Indeed, sir," Torsen quickly replied. "We have five special ops bears in the grizzly country of Beyond the Beyond."

"But our bears are white, and the bears of the south are brown or black," Hvrak, an Issengard, said. "Do they not stand out?"

A twinkle sparkled in Edith's dark eyes. "They are no longer white, sir. We have obtained—by means I cannot reveal—dyes. Their pelts have been stained a dark brown, the same color as the grizzlies' fur."

And their tongues? thought Galilya. *Have you dyed their blue tongues red?* For blue was the color of the white bears of the Nunquivik's tongues and their skin beneath the fur was black as night.

"Then go, go and destroy these four bears." The Grand Patek rose. "Look up! Look through the portal in this hallowed chamber at the claws of the Great Ursus constellation as it rises on this night to bless our mission." So great was the agitation of the Grand Patek that the air was flecked with spittle as he spoke. "We shall cut a swath of blood across their lands. Remember, strength lies not in defense but attack! The struggle is ours. It is the means by which we shall rise against all creatures and the most brutal struggles will raise us even higher. Our time is approaching. The calculations tell us that the conditions for the great release are approaching. The punishment will commence in the Moon of the First Cracks!" His eyes were rolling back in his head as he shook his clawed fist at the fist of the Great Ursus constellation.

Is this monster bear challenging the stars? Galilya's mind roiled.

As the spotted owl was escorted from the chamber, Galilya glanced at Udo, the Master of the Pendulum, and her one ally in the clock. How they had worked with those coded equations to slow the flow to the bungvik and avert the impending disaster of its flooding and the ultimate destruction of the great regions of Ga'Hoole. Did Udo suspect her true nature?

There was, however, a new alertness in the chamber as two Issengards returned from escorting the spotted owl from the chamber. It was highly unusual that Issengards would return like this. They normally stood guard outside the chamber except when delivering a visitor. The visitor had been delivered. Why would they now return? Something did not feel right.

The Grand Patek was back on his ice throne. He sighed, seeming slightly depleted from his rant. His dark gaze swept the chamber. "Servants of the clock, wise bears of the Gilraan, I have yet another announcement to make. It is with a great and heavy heart that I must declare that a traitor sits among us." Fear flashed through the chamber like the cutting wind of the blynd-spryee. *Impossible*, thought Galilya. *Have they discovered that I'm a . . .* She couldn't complete the thought. "Will our faithful and wise Chronos identify this traitor?" Galilya felt her stomach churn as she watched the smug bear Torsenvryk Torsen seated next to her rise from the bench and in the company of the two Issengard make his way to the end of the bench, where Udo, the Master of the Pendulum, was seated. Galilya's heart seized. Would she be next? Those last coded computations they had done together were enough to condemn both of them. There was a huge ice-shaking roar as Master Udo leaped to his feet.

But it was too late. A snare of nets had dropped from the sky port. The largest of the Issengard bears were hauling him off the bench. He was soon dangling in the air just beneath the sky port. Galilya looked up. She saw the elaborate pulley system attached to an ice jack and a crane for lifting very large chunks and floes of ice to fortify the clock base. However, the crane was now lifting Udo. She sensed what would happen. He would be dropped, not pushed like the old Chronos from the highest parapet.

The Grand Patek began to speak.

"The Master of the Pendulum, Udo Einharr, has been found guilty of heresy and highest treason to the clock by deliberately falsifying calculations to indicate that our great Ice Clock is churning." There was no way Galilya was going to escape. They would not drop him, she realized now, but most likely take him to a black ice ort and torture him until he revealed any accomplices. And then she would be killed. Unless . . . she shifted. Unless she became a fox again.

I am who I am. The words thundered in her head like an approaching storm.

The meeting of the Gilraan in the Stellata chamber was adjourned. Galilya rushed to her ice den. She had thought she had to stay to somehow slow the clock, but that was not going to work if the Grand Patek really had the great release set for the Moon of the First Cracks. When had he decided this? He was in fact following a set of lunar calculations. She must escape through the secret panel in her own small harmonics lab. She went into the lab. But first she would begin her transformation. She would do it right. She would do it completely. She would not rush it. She regarded her shadow cast on the white wall of the ice. She felt the strange music that always came with the transformation rise within her. She sensed her body begin to shrink, her legs grow shorter, and a pulse click in her paws. The sparkling line of the Northing illuminated her mind. Her ears pricked. There was suddenly a sound at the entry to her den, but she was here, tucked away safe. Then there was the luxuriant swish of her tail sweeping the ice. But more sounds outside the harmonics lab were those of footsteps, heavy footsteps coming closer as the music of her true soul rose within her.

"Galilya!" It was Torsen. "Heart of my heart! Where are . . . are . . . you?" he stammered as he caught sight of a fox and staggered a bit.

She wheeled about and sprang through the opening where Torsen stood. His eyes did not believe the sight in front of him. She had but one chance. She sprang as only a Nunquivik fox could, landing on his chest and sinking her fangs into Torsen's neck.

He fell to the ground. A great pool of blood was forming. It would soon seep into the corridor outside her den. Galilya wasted no time. She dashed back to the harmonics lab, gave a light push to the ice panel, and began sliding through the interior tunnels. Within less than a minute, she was back on the ice banks of the small pond where Jameson had died and the very spot where Svenna had knocked her senseless. But now her senses had returned. She began swimming just as Svenna had, but unlike Svenna, Galilya knew her way through the dangerous maze of gears and baffles. *I am who I am!* The words roared in her head.

CHAPTER 16

Ambush in Ambala

The four yosses now threaded their way through a wooded area. The ground was spongy with moss. Night was falling, and the starlight trickled down through the canopy of trees. They might have been tired, but their nerves propelled them. What would these creatures so new to them be like? If there were slipgizzles and hireclaws about, and if they had heard that the key had been delivered to the Great Tree, war could come sooner than expected. Each yoss had its own particular anxieties, but Stellan felt his most acutely. He, after all, was the frynmater, the diplomat. What if he made an error in the intricate protocol that was required of him? Used a wrong word with the wolves or an incorrect posture? There was a very intricate way in which one was supposed to greet a wolf, particularly the chieftain of a clan.

Why didn't Da tell us about this possibility of war? Stellan thought as they finally settled down, exhausted, to catch a short nap.

"Oh no!" a voice moaned.

"'Oh no' what?" Third asked.

"You're all growing sleepy. You're so boring when you sleep," Rags whined.

"Perhaps we are," Stellan said, and began to yawn as well. "Funny how quickly we've gone back to our old bear ways."

"Well, I haven't," Rags said petulantly.

"Of course not, Rags, but while we sleep, you can practice your flying and your hunting," Froya said.

"I almost caught that mole back there."

"Then keep trying," Third said, and began to curl up on a pad of moss that was just the perfect size.

"All right."

Rags flew low, just above the forest floor, scanning the ground for the telltale swells of the mole's underground tunnel. It took her a bit of time to pick up the mole's trail. As she flew, she was bemoaning the fact that, unlike other owlets, she had had no one to teach her how to track. She had come to love the bears dearly, and she in fact owed her newly acquired flight skills to them, for she had learned to fly by first hopping off the tops of their heads from one to another. It wasn't that different from the branching that owlets did under their parents' supervision when they would hop from limb to limb in a tree getting ready for their first real flights. When Rags would begin to plummet, it was always a soft landing into the bears' plush fur. A nice soft crash. But she knew she had to learn kill spirals and power dives to become a real hunter. And the bears weren't much use for that.

Suddenly, she spied the swollen track of a mole tunnel. Now, how to lure the creature out? At the very same moment, a furry little ball emerged from a mound at the end of the track. *That's it!* A thousand thoughts rushed through Rags's head. *I'm flying too low for the kill spiral . . . too low for any kind of power dive.* The creature turned toward her and began quivering. *It's blind. It can't see me, but it knows I'm here. Don't think—just DO!!!* Rags accelerated and flew straight toward the creature. She extended her talons and sank them into the mole's back. Blood spurted. The creature struggled. She sank her talons in deeper. Together they rolled across the top of the mole's tunnel. With her beak, she began to tear through the fur. More blood, and then the mole went limp. *It's dead. I killed it!*

This was her first real kill. Until now, she had to be satisfied with worms and grubs and fish the bears caught in the creeks. *I should be having my first kill ceremony.* And what happened to her first flight ceremony? That was what owl families always did. She knew from hearing owls that had dwelled in nearby tree hollows talk about it. All those creatures, however, left by the time Rags's mum, Edith, had left. Rags had never thought about it before, but she wondered now why they had all left. All those parents had taken their owlets with them. Only she had been left behind—alone. *Orphaned,* that was the word Rabbit had used. It meant left, in Rags's mind. Left behind. Never to catch up. It meant unloved! And now here she was in the woods, staring down at her first real kill. *I'll have to do these ceremonies all by myself . . . What would the bears know about it?* She began to cry into the bloody little mess on the ground in front of her. She sighed. She recalled the words of the song she had heard coming from another hollow of a whiskered screech when their owlets had their first fur-on-meat-with-bones ceremony. She hadn't heard the song for the kill ceremony, but this one would do, wouldn't it?

"Well, here goes," she muttered, and began to sing.

The fur will tickle
The blood will trickle
And the tail we'll pickle
Just for you
Oh, little owl
Let us all hoot
And give a fine salute
For your first fur on meat
A most delicious treat!

There was more to the song, but Rags couldn't remember it and somehow singing it all alone in this woods made her even sadder. She would tell the bears about it when she returned. But she had promised, sworn on her gizzard, that she would not wake them until dawn. Of course, then she would be sleepy and curl up on one of their heads, or in the thick fur on the backs of their necks and snooze while they made their way to the Brad at the very center of Ambala.

Third, sleeping on a broad cushion of moss, was lost in a dream. It was a dream of strange colors and odd scents. But he couldn't attach these smells and hues to anything that he knew. Yet there was a peculiar familiarity. There was also an indefinable sense of dread. Dread and darkness, as if a shadow was stalking him; not just him, but all of them. Now he felt something shaking him.

"Get up. It's dawn, and Rags has some exciting news to tell us. She is almost bursting."

Third roused himself. Blinked several times. Through the trees, he could glimpse fragments of the horizon quivering with dusty pinks and oranges.

"I have an announcement to make," Rags said, swooping back and forth in dizzying loops in front of the bleary eyes of the bears.

"Yes?" Stellan tried to muster some enthusiasm, although he could have slept a bit longer. It was barely dawn.

Rags settled on a stump. "I have killed a mole."

"So you found it?" Third said, now fully awake. "I thought you would."

"Yes, but you know what that means?"

"A milestone of sorts, I guess," Third said.

"Uh, we call them flight marks I think, actually kind of two flight marks. I never had a first fur-on-bones ceremony and now a first kill."

"Ceremonies?" Froya said.

Rags felt something beginning to cave inside her. They didn't understand. She began to quiver a bit. Stellan immediately sensed her despair. This was a most significant flight mark for owls. Yes, he was sure, and they were completely ignorant.

"Yes, there are ceremonies, and I did the ceremony all by myself in the woods where I found the mole and . . . sang the song . . . and . . ." Rags was trembling.

Stellan thought his own heart would break.

"Well, Rags, you must sing it again for us, right now, right here where we stand." The other bears were ashamed of their own ignorance. They should have known after their time at the tree how important ceremonies were in the lives of owls.

"Yes, do sing it!" Jytte said.

Froya and Third clapped their paws. "Sing. Sing!"

"All right," Rags said, and flying up to a higher branch in the tree that hung out just over where the bears stood, she began to sing the song once more. When she had finished, she flew back to the stump and dipped as if taking a bow.

"And," Stellan said, "I bet, I just bet, there is a first flight ceremony and a song to go with that."

Rags twisted her head a bit and buried her beak shyly in her shoulder feathers. "Well, actually, yes, there is."

"Would you sing that one?" Jytte asked.

"Please! Please!" Froya and Third both begged.

"All right. But I must sing it while flying. I mean, usually the parents of the owlet sing it to them while flying but . . . well, you know."

"Believe me, Rags," Stellan said, "if we could fly alongside you, we would."

"Thank you," Rags said softly. "You're the best!" And with that, she swooped into the air.

I never stop to bid the earth good-bye
As I escape to the sky
The stars are mine to embrace
The dark of night is mine to taste
The air is for my wings to bite
On this, my very first ever flight
At times a cloud does appear
At times the air is scraped with sleet
But I carve the wind
My wings do beat
I carve the rain
And come back again,
My first flight is not my last
My shadow against the moon is cast

Third listened to the last line of the song. It was as if a shadow slid across his own mind. He could not shake the shards of that dream that dug into him sharp as hyivqik ice. It was the smell that troubled him like no scent he had ever encountered, or could even imagine. How could dreams have a scent to smell?

They had been walking for several hours when they realized that they had taken a wrong turn and were now backtracking. Third stopped suddenly, so suddenly that his sister, Froya, bumped into him.

"What is it?" she asked.

"That smell." Froya lifted he muzzle and sniffed the air. "Do you smell it, Froya?"

"I do smell something, but it's . . . it's . . ."

"Not like anything you ever smelled. Right?"

She nodded. Then Stellan turned. "I smell something very strange."

"Me too," said Jytte. At that moment, a dark bear emerged from a thicket of brambles. Then a second and a third followed. *Our first grizzlies!* thought Jytte. They were larger than she had expected, for she recalled the bears of the Beyond were supposed to be smaller than those of the Nunquivik. It was difficult for Jytte to read the expressions in their faces. This was like looking into a night fog, or *nacht nieblen*, a condition that occured in the Nunquivik when the sea ice began to smoke.

Jytte's right, Stellan thought. They are larger than we thought . . . but . . . well, he was the frynmater, the diplomat. So he stepped forward on all fours and scraped his muzzle to the ground, which was the common etiquette to both the bears of the Nunquivik and those of the Beyond, then spoke.

"Grizzlies, I assume from the kingdom known as Beyond the Beyond?" *Why are they still standing up straight?* he wondered, but persisted. "We know about you. Yes, we studied you. We share many of your same customs of greeting, or so I thought." His muzzle was still touching the ground. The bears said nothing but merely nodded. It was as if Stellan were reciting his essay from the final test they took before they had left the Great Ga'Hoole Tree. Third was stiff with fear. He extended a paw to caution Stellan. Something was not right here. Why were these bears so silent? And the smell! Suddenly, he knew what it was. It was their fur. Their fur had been dyed. There was only one place where these bears could have obtained such dyes. The kraals! *Kraal* was the old Krakish word for the pirate owls of the Northern Kingdoms! They had a long history in the Hrathlands. Svern had told them about the kraals but said that most of them had vanished after the last big owl war, the War of the Ember. Their dye basins, however, had been left behind. The basins were shallow spots near a region pocked with smee holes, or steam vents. It was the steam that kept the basins percolating with their colorful liquids. Svern, of course, would know all about this being a spy, for Yinquis used old dried-out steam holes for listening. The sound transmission was perfect for their listening activities and tapping out coded messages. Like hireclaws, the kraals fought for no particular kingdom.

These bears who stood before them had obviously soaked themselves in the pots to change the color of their fur and to camouflage themselves as grizzlies of the Beyond. But beneath those dyes they were as white as Third.

Stellan was staring at Third, riddling his thoughts. Was it possible these brown-furred bears were actually Roguers from the Nunquivik? That they were already here in the Southern Kingdoms of Ga'Hoole? There was a second gesture of greeting that friendly bears used when approaching each other. They signaled their friendliness by turning their paws inward so their claws did not face out and bumped their paws softly against each other. He would try. Stellan began to do just this to the closest bear. The bear shrank back and accidentally bumped against Jytte's arm.

"What's this?" She looked at the dark stain. Trying to comprehend what she sensed but at the same time trying to resist the truth. These bears were white. White as any bear from the Nunquivik—*but not any bear. Roguer bears, all of them!* The truth seared across her brain like a blazing comet in the night sky during a Blood Moon.

The largest bear roared, opening his mouth. His fangs were like no fangs they had ever seen but jagged like the teeth of an escapement wheel of a timepiece. The teeth on which so many cubs had died. The bear lunged forward.

The jagged fangs flashed in the moonlight. Roaring shook the forest as this bear swung at Froya. Jytte leaped onto another one's back and began to furiously bite its ear. The bear yowled. Rags flew to a high branch out of the reach of the tallest bear and watched the fight in horror. The dark bears were outnumbered, but they were bigger and fierce. And they all had those fangs. The yosses, however, were light on their feet and quicker.

"Watch your back, Froya. Your back!" Rags shrieked. Froya wheeled about quickly and then somersaulted out of the path of the advancing bear. The bear looked stunned. He tipped his head up toward the branch where Rags perched. The little spotted owl realized that this indeed was her chance. *Kill spiral!* It was an instantaneous power dive. Her spots blurred as she whistled down. Extending her talons, she aimed for the bear's eyes.

The bear was bellowing in pain, but all three now began running. One of the bears roared back. "The key for this bear! Where is the key?"

What was the bear talking about? They all wondered. How did these bears know about the key?

Then Froya shrieked as the meaning became clear.

"They got Third. They got my brother!" She froze as she imagined those fangs devouring him. Stellan was almost paralyzed, caught between his own horror and the vivid images in Third being devoured. *They've taken Third hostage for the key!*

Jytte broke the spell. "After them!" Her scream split the air.

The three yosses tore through the night. Their fear melted away in the hot flash of their anger. Stellan felt a fury in his chest that burned like fire.

But Roguer bears were fast. And they seemed to know where they were going. It began to sleet and then soon was raining heavily. Within a few leagues, the yosses had lost their track and the sharp scent of the dyes had disappeared. They tried to continue, but by the time the moon slipped away, they realized they had been going in circles.

"We've lost them," Froya sobbed, and came to an abrupt stop.

"I'm not stopping," Rags said. "I'll have more chance of finding them than you."

"But it's dark," Froya cried.

"I'm an owl, for Glaux's sake. I am born for the black of the night—any night. I can cover more distance flying than you ever could walking."

"All right!" Stellan said. "Jytte, you head this way." He pointed to the north. "Froya, you head that way. And I'll go ahead. We'll meet back here when . . ."

"When the moon passes Grank's Anvil," Froya said, pointing up at the constellation of the legends.

But Rags paid them no heed. They were land creatures bound to earth. She could fly to Grank's Anvil three times and back before the moon passed. So instead, the tiny owl, who had only taken wing in the last few days, flew through the rest of the night, into the dawn, and greeted Joss, the morning star, before she returned and was utterly exhausted.

"Nothing," the spotted owl said, and collapsed. Night was falling again, and now she was too tired to do anything.

"You tried," Froya sobbed, and patted Rags's head. "You tried."

CHAPTER 17

A Code Is Cracked!

Svenna was heading south by southwest, cutting across the ice of the vast Nunqua Sea. It seemed like Great Ursus had blessed this journey of escape, as the wind was at her back. Her plan was to go to the Northern Kingdoms of Ga'Hoole. She was sure Svern was there. She had overheard that a renowned Yinqui had escaped from one of the Roguer torture cells. And if it was Svern, he would have headed to the Northern Kingdoms. Of this she was certain. Perhaps the cubs had somehow found their way to him. Second, now Jytte, according the Jameson the seal, had always been so curious about their father. Much more so than First, now Stellan. Jytte asked endless questions about where he might be. Why did father bears never stay with their young? She was so determined and at the same time so impulsive she could imagine Jytte talking Stellan into finding their da. So perhaps that was where she should head—to the Firth of Grundensphyrr, where they had first met in the Northern Kingdoms, or perhaps to Stormfast Island, where Svern had come from.

She recalled now Jameson's words as he lay dying. *They were well . . . and they have names . . . Jytte and Stellan.* She treasured those ten words. They were as precious as any jewels.

With that favorable wind came the heavy blizzards of the jumble moon, quickly erasing her tracks. A blessing in itself, but of course the stars were also wiped away. Although she was not an ice gazer like her daughter, Jytte, she did possess certain sensibilities about snow. She could tell that there was more moisture in the air as she traveled south. Did she feel slight vibrations beneath the snow? She took one of her broad paws and began to scrape. It was deep and she had to scrape for a while, but finally the ice was clear of snow. Crouching down, she pressed her port ear to the exposed ice sheet and heard it—the rustling waters of the N'yrthghar Straits.

"I'm coming home!" she whispered to herself in wonder. "I'm coming home!"

By first light, which was just a squeak of pink on the horizon, she turned into the straits, which were not completely frozen. "My, my," she said softly. "Things have certainly been rearranged here." She looked about and realized a large portion of the Hrath'ghar Glacier must have torn loose in an avalanche. The familiar contours of the coastline had been completely rejiggered. New bays cut out, old bays filled with the ice sopple, the trash from a glacier on the move—chunks of rock, trees, whatever was in its path. She studied this new landscape for a while and then swam on.

Within a few hours, she would find the Bay of Fangs. She made her way up toward the Firth of Grundensphyrr, then turned west. She was tired by now, and straight ahead she saw the old dye pots of the kraals. It had been years since the kraals had lived here, but a few of their pots were still simmering, fed by the underground steam vents. She wandered through. She had passed a bright yellow one, and nearby a green one. Farther away, she spied the signs of an old steam vent. She wondered if a Yinqui had ever used it or perhaps was now using it as a listening station. She slowed her pace. As she came closer, she saw splatters of blue and orange dyes. There was one basin where it looked as if the two colors had been combined, for around the edges were splashes of very dark blue and orange. But in the basin itself was a pool of brown dye. There were footprints around the pool— bear footprints. Then, just ahead, she spotted splashes of red dye.

Svenna scratched her head in confusion. *What happened here?* she wondered. She felt her heartbeat quicken. Something was not right. A peculiar odor cut through the splatters of the dye. Horrified, she realized that the red was not dye at all but blood. Ahead she saw a huge mound. Cautiously she approached. It was a bear, a dead bear. A murdered bear. There were bear claw marks all over him. His blood had congealed in the snow. There were also smears of brown, the brown dye she had just passed by in the basin. Svenna could tell that he had been dead for some time—perhaps half a moon. In addition to the bear claw marks, there was the unmistakable evidence of vultures. With their beaks and talons, the scavenger birds had torn at the wounds. She walked around, slowly examining the bear tracks, the splashes of dye and blood on the ground. The kraals might be gone, but something worse had arrived. Then it dawned on Svenna. This victim was most likely a Yinqui. Had he been dragged from his listening post at one of the dried-out smee holes? The region must be pocked with smee holes. Many had probably dried out. Hadn't Svern once mentioned how prolific smee holes were in this region? That it was perfect for Yinquis? She had to find the smee hole from which this bear had transmitted. In that moment, she felt a welter of emotions boil up inside of her. She clamped her eyes shut and thought of Svern. Was he alive? Dead? Or, she prayed, perhaps he was in one of his Yinqui dens, somewhere, someplace?

On the island of Stormfast, winter had come with a ferocity not usually known in these parts. Svern was in the listening nook of his Yinqui post, tapping out for perhaps the fifth time an encrypted message to his paw master, code-named Blue Bear, who was stationed in Lower Rainbow, a code name for the region that the kraals used to occupy. For a Yinqui, it was an ideal location due to its good smee holes. Terrific transmitting ice from the Hrath'ghar Glacier and a good observation point to the north and east. But Blue Bear had not responded, and now Svern was getting nervous. He, of course, thanked Ursus that messages had been getting through between himself and Blythe at the Great Tree. She had assured him that not only had the yosses arrived and proved to be excellent students, but were now on a mission to recruit allies. He knew this recruitment mission was a possibility and would be a shock to the young bears. But it was typical of the owls to work this way. He had been reluctant to tell them this before their departure, as it might be too disheartening to them. They had to go forward with this mission with confidence.

In any case, at the moment, he was quite disheartened himself at the silence from Blue Bear. What did it mean? It was Blue Bear who had recruited him long ago as a Yinqui and taught Svern everything he knew about Yinqui craft. Without his paw master reporting on enemy movement, he felt as though he had been left dangling. But he was going to have to stop transmitting. Too many repeated coded messages that went unanswered were risky. He would have to cross this Yinqui post off. It was simply too dangerous to keep it up. An enemy bear could pick up on it. Although they were unschooled in code, if there was excessive transmitting they might be able to detect the origins. A good Yinqui was chary in his or her transmissions, only transmitting when absolutely necessary and with the briefest of messages. They changed posts often. The den from which Svern was transmitting was not the same one he had shown the yosses. He decided to try Blue Bear one more time. Nothing came back, and he began to doze. Like soft vapors, thoughts and images of

Svenna began to stir in his mind. She was a good bear, a smart bear, and so beautiful. She was of the Sven clan, the same clan as the hero bear Svenka. They of all the clans had the closest relationship with the owls of the Northern Kingdoms. Svenka had been responsible for saving Queen Siv after she had been wounded by a hagsfiend. It was rumored that the Guardian owls had a portrait of Svenka at the Great Tree.

Svenna, the descendent of Svenka, had the most beautiful dark eyes, which possessed an almost amber cast. And so he called her *likki*, for there was one shade in the ahalikki lights that was the same color, and they together had danced beneath that amber light the first time they had met and she called him *kaeru*, which meant dear one. They were their secret names for each other, their *leyn navn*. They had danced to the music of the ahalikki, which only bears could sometimes hear—it was a music of color and wind.

He had nodded off and on the near edge of a beautiful dream—the undulating lights of the ahalikki and the amber eyes of his beloved Svenna. What he would give to hear her call out to him *kaeru . . . kaeru min elskede*—dear one, dear one, my beloved. A sob swelled in him like a breaking wave from the Everwinter Sea. Something seemed to scratch at his dream like claws against the music of the ahalikki. It was a most unmusical sound. Svern was awake instantly. Could it be his paw master, Blue Bear? He tapped back, giving his own code name. But the response was not what he wanted. It was not a confirmation.

"Code name," he tapped: —** . . . **

The response made no sense at all. Whoever was at the other end was trying but was completely untutored. Or was this a ruse of some sort? A trick? Was he being lured into something? Then he had this mysterious inkling. Just a glimmer, really. Although he was a coder, he had never thought of himself as having gifts like his cubs: Stellan, a riddler of minds, and Jytte, an ice gazer. But suddenly it was as if he sensed the mind of the bear at the source of the tapping. *Impossible!* he thought. It couldn't be. And then he remembered he had taught Svenna the tapping codes for their names. It was a simple code. Not based on the poems of Ezylryb but of their secret names. He now tapped out the symbols for *Likki*: ⇔••⇔. Svern held his breath. He waited. It was not long before the first tap came through. ΠΘΣϖξ. He gasped in disbelief. *Kaeru!* It was Svenna! "Svenna!" he cried out, and tears poured down his face.

CHAPTER 18

Of Scrooms and Moonlight

Third did not squirm or wiggle or yell out. There was no use. These were three powerful bears. The wounded one was no longer bleeding, so that meant the trail would not be so easily followed. But would Stellan, Jytte, and Froya follow? It was not that he doubted their loyalty. In fact, he hoped they would follow, but should they first go to the Brad and get help from the greenowls of Ambala? However, at this moment, Third was unsure if he was even still in the territory of Ambala. The tiny bear felt his heart race, and his breath became short, as if he couldn't catch it. As if there was not enough air for him to breathe. Panic surged in him like a rising tide. *We have all of us gone through so much—am I now to die? Shall I never see Froya, Jytte, Stellan . . . again?*

He had to stop thinking such thoughts. He looked about. Was there any way he could escape? These bears were huge.

Stellan might have been able to fight them off, but he was locked in the grip of the largest one, who was dragging him across a rutted landscape. Each time he tried to twist out of the grip, the bear tightened his paw. The pain was excruciating. He could hardly breathe. Would they really kill him if they didn't get the key? He had to think, but he could hardly think.

"Let up a bit," he gasped. "If I die, you're never going to get the key."

"Oh, they'll get it." An owl swooped down. "We have our methods."

"Hireclaw scum!" Third shot back.

The owl darted in and gave him a sharp peck on his head with her beak. Third refused to cry out. Let them tear him apart. He would not waste a breath. He couldn't waste a breath. He had to focus on breathing more steadily, more slowly, not tearing at the air as if it were raw seal meat. Slow but steady, that was what he must do. He was small, he knew it. He was scared. But he had to think, save his energy, and somehow, some way, he had to escape.

He had no idea where he was being taken. They had barely talked. But he had a feeling that the owl was directing them, showing them the way. The terrain had shifted. The ground was harder, rockier. There was nothing green, and the trees grew sparser. They appeared to be entering an entirely new landscape. Slender needles of rock thrust up into the dark and starry night. They were passing through a canyon bristling with stone. This must be the Canyonlands of St. Aegolius, a place of infamy in owl history. They had learned about it from their lessons with Otulissa. This was where the treacherous owls known as Pure Ones had dwelled and kept captive young owlets they had seized, owlnapped to serve in their wars. Soren and his friend Gylfie, an elf owl, had been snatched as very young owlets.

Third and his captors were now winding their way through a maze of narrow canyon passageways. It became apparent to Third that the spotted owl was leading them by flying just a few feet above the ground. Every now and then, she swiveled her head or flipped it entirely. She would call out, "Still with me?"

"Yes!" the lead bear would call back.

And then, finally, they were in a very small but deep box canyon. It was beginning to blaze with moonlight. The spotted owl perched on an outcropping. In that moment, Third realized that this owl bore a very strong resemblance to Rags. Could this be the mother who had left her?

"All right, bears." The owl began to speak. "We are in a very special place at a very special time of this particular moon. It is what we call full shine. There was a custom here known as moon blinking. I think you will find that it is as effective as your black ice orts for extracting information." The owl glared at Third.

"Where are the torture instruments?" asked a bear who the others had addressed as Alfghar. Third felt now as if the air was being sucked out of him. He had to resist but could he? Could mysterious forces of moonlight destroy his mind? He had read about this method of torture at the Great Tree. It was bloodless.

There was no pain—only the ghastly sensation of one's mind being taken over, invaded, and becoming a toy for evil forces to manipulate.

"Right up there!" The owl pointed cheerfully. "Let this fellow bake out here under the moon for a few hours." Third knew what was coming. *And he'll be moon blinked.* "Yes, once he's under the spell of the moon's light, he'll tell you all you need to know about the whereabouts of the key. His brain will become mush. Pliable. He will tell whatever you demand. The exact location of the key in the Great Tree."

But I don't even know it, Third thought.

Again, the owl turned to Third. "You will be completely under their command, with no will of your own." She seemed to derive some perverse enjoyment as she spoke these words.

So how can I tell them if I don't know? Third wondered. Perhaps he should say this? *Perhaps not!* These bears were fools. *And maybe,* Third thought, *I can fool them.*

"You're sure of this, Edith? That is your name?"

"It is, but I prefer to be addressed as agent Point 09."

"Of course." Another bear nodded, the one whom they had referred to as Alfghar.

"But how do we guard him while protecting ourselves?" asked Fyor, the bear whose face had been slashed by Rags's talons. One eye was swollen shut. "And as you can see, I'm not much good for keeping watch."

"Yes, I was going to ask who attacked your eye."

"Actually, an owl similar to yourself. But smaller."

"A spotted owl?" Edith asked. A shiver ran through her as she felt her gizzard clench. She wilfed a bit and appeared to grow smaller before the bears.

"Well, don't worry," Edith said. "There are only two entrances into the moon chamber, as the owls called it back in the day of St. Aegolius Academy. There are three of you, so you can guard them easily. You must not, however, come into the chamber, for the moon will be directly overhead within the next few minutes."

"Three minutes, forty-five seconds, and two milliseconds," Svorg, the third bear, answered.

It always amazed Edith how these bears could keep such precise track of time. "As you say," she continued mildly. "The point is, you should by no means step into this chamber during those long minutes when the moon is directly overhead. A glaring light will fill this space, and you shall instantly become moon blinked. However, as soon as the moon passes and when the light begins to slant, then, as it sinks in the western sky, you can reenter safely." Edith paused, then turned to Third. "And you, your brains shall be slop!"

They all left. Third tipped his head back. The moon was sailing overhead on its inexorable path. What would it feel like to have your mind, your will, destroyed? Should he cover his eyes? And what about that part of his mind that walked through dreams? Would it be wrecked? He felt as if he was about to be annihilated, so vandalized that he would not even recognize himself.

Third saw the deadly silver disc of the moon begin to creep over the edge of the high rock walls. Panic filled him again. He began to gasp as though he were drowning, but not in water. Suffocating not from lack of air, but rather light. He was being devoured by a terrible light. It cut through him with bright glittering fangs. He was losing consciousness. Third felt himself crumple into a corner of the chamber. His head dropped listlessly to one side, resting on his shoulder. The last flicker of a tiny flame within him was being doused, and that flicker was his mind.

There was a fluttering in the air. Something cool began to steal over him. He opened his eyes. He felt just as he had before the moon had scalded his brain. He could recall the dream he'd had of the strange smell, the dyes of the bears who had carried him off. He could still smell them, for they were right outside. The light-bleached chamber was dim now. But what was all this fluttering?

"Owls?" he whispered.

"Not exactly," a voice said.

"Haven't I been moon blinked?"

"Not at all," chirped another voice. But was there more than one?

"Where are you? . . . I see shadows of you . . . but . . . but . . ."

"But not us, right?"

"Yes," Third said.

"We're scrooms," said another, and this time a misty figure seemed to hover in the air. It had all the appearances of a barn owl with its white heart-shaped face. "We're spirits, sort of like your gillygaskins, the ones who have not quite made it all the way to your bear heaven."

"Ursulana?" Third asked.

"Yes," replied another owl. Its piercing bright yellow eyes peered out from a face of concentric gray and white circles. "Except we call it glaumora."

"But why aren't you there?" Third asked.

"Well," said another. A tiny elf owl. "There are some of us that have formed a brigade, a ghost army so to speak. We revisit on the nights of a full shine moon, to rescue any creature who has been trapped, accidentally perhaps, or on purpose, as in your case, to be blistered and blinked by the moon. It had happened to us long ago. And we took a vow to try not to ever let it happen again. But this is the first time in a long time that another species—bears—have brought their own kind here."

"We blame it on Edith," the barn owl said.

"But you have saved me from being moon blinked. I'm not sure how exactly, but how will I leave? There are three bears out there waiting to torture me."

"Moon blinked," said the elf owl in a matter-of-fact tone.

"Huh?"

"We moon blinked them," replied the great gray. "We absorbed all the moonlight. We as scrooms can no longer be affected by such exposure, but we can expose others by spraying them with the light we absorbed."

"Fascinating!" Third said in awe.

"We hovered in front of them. They are deeply blinked now. When they awake, their brains will not function."

"Not properly at least," added the barn owl. "They will stagger around in these canyons for several days and not even know why they came in the first place, or where they are going."

"And me, how do I get out?"

"Easy enough," the elf owl said. "We'll guide you toward wherever you want to go."

"The Brad!"

"Ah yes, the Brad!" they repeated, and churred.

"The greenowls of Ambala," the great gray added.

"Indeed!"

"Then follow us," said the barn owl.

Third walked out from the stone enclosure, stepping over the unconscious bodies of the three bears. How stupid they looked with their brown-stained fur and yet their blue tongues hanging out. The scrooms spread their wings and lifted into the air. They appeared in the night like glowing spheres of mist with silvery wings. *Like the stars*, Third thought. He trusted these three scrooms to guide him like the stars.

The yosses were growing more desperate. Three times they had set out in separate directions, only to circle back to their meeting place each time with nothing to report. Nor had Rags anything to report.

"We need a new plan!" Jytte said grumpily. "This is complete nonsense."

Stellan sighed. "Well, what would you suggest that would not be 'nonsense,' Jytte?"

"Don't make fun of me. I hate it when you do that." Rags regarded the two arguing bears and glanced nervously at Froya, who seemed to be growing more and more desperate.

"Do what?" Stellan shot back.

"You know! You do it all the time in that superior way of yours."

"STOP IT!" Froya shouted. "This is not a sibling squabble. My sibling is lost and you two arguing gets us nowhere."

"What do you suggest?" Jytte asked in a somewhat calmer tone.

"I suggest that we go to the Brad. That we ask the greenowls."

"That is a plan," Stellan said.

"Yes, that is a plan," Jytte agreed, suddenly docile.

Froya now took out her star map and studied it silently. She had already plotted a course to the Brad, which at this time of the night in the Moon of the Copper-Rose Rain would be directly beneath the second star of the Great Glaux constellation.

"This way," Froya said quietly, and began to lead the way, with Jytte and Stellan dropping in behind her.

They traveled on until they grew tired and decided to take just the briefest of rests.

"Maybe here," Rags suggested. "Under this tree. You know it's a full shine moon and that can be dangerous for owls."

"Oh, moon blinking," Stellan said. "Yes, we heard about that. Mostly I believe it happens when one is in a confined space. But this is quite nice." He looked up through the spreading shadows of a tangle of limbs at the full shine moon.

Sleep, however, was not the bears' friend tonight. Nor was it Rags's friend. She tossed and turned and cursed herself for losing the trail of those horrible bears. Finally, knowing that she had a better chance than the bears with her view from above, she quietly set out from her roost in a tree.

Earlier, Rags had been rather haphazard in her approach to tracking the horrid bears. But now she decided to try a more methodical approach. She would use this slender fir tree as her base, then fly out in a different direction each time. She looked up at the sky. The moon was dipping down in the west on its way to Beyond the Beyond, where the wolf clans lived. The Golden Talons were rising in the east, and just above was the Great Glaux constellation. She flew east in setting her course by the starboard wing of the Great Glaux. Skimming low over a grove of birch trees, she tried to pick up any sign that bears had passed through. There was none, not a hint of that vile scent of the dyes they had used to stain their fur. She knew there had been something wrong as soon as she caught a glimpse of one of those terrible bears. What other creature on earth had a blue tongue? When she had first met the yosses, while they were sleeping at night, she would often tiptalon to see if perhaps one or two of them slept with their tongues hanging out. Jytte often did. She had never met a creature with a blue tongue. All the birds she knew, not many, but owls certainly, had pink tongues. Nest-maid snakes as well. Although her mum never had a nest-maid snake. "What do we need a snake slithering around our hollow for? Just a bunch of old gossips," she would mutter when she heard other owls talking about nest-maid snakes.

Rags had just finished making her fourth foray out from the tree and come back to rest when she saw that the branch she had perched on was already occupied by another owl. A spotted owl. As she drew closer, she began to stall in her flight. Her eyes opened wide in utter shock.

"Mum!"

"Not me!" the owl squawked back.

"But it is you, Mum. I'd recognize you anywhere."

"Scram." The owl lifted off the branch and in a twisting flight surged high into the air. Then she began a hurtling plunge. *A kill spiral! My mum is in a kill spiral and coming for me!*

Rags's wings locked. She began plummeting to the ground. The last thing she remembered was a green flash in the night.

CHAPTER 19

The Greenowls of Ambala

Deep in the most enchanting part of the forest of Ambala was the Brad. A special place where the owls gathered nightly before taking flight and then reassembling at twixt time as the dawn broke. There they would exchange stories and sometimes recite verses from their favorite books they had rescued during the hideous reign of the infamous Blue Striga, a dragon owl from the Middle Kingdom who began to burn the precious books and volumes of the Great Tree. The owls of Ambala had rescued many of these books. The Blue Striga and his "storm owls" were finally decimated. But during the time of their dominion, the greenowls of Ambala began to memorize as many books as possible before they were destroyed. These owls were now gathered around the glowing coals from the blacksmith of Ambala. It was a sight that Stellan would long remember, as impressive as the parliament of the owls, yet different. Every single owl from the largest, a great gray, to the smallest, a tiny northern saw-whet, wore a mantle of green moss across its shoulders. These owls seemed almost like spirits of this forest, as if they had been perhaps born from the deep greenness of the trees and the very texture of leaves and lichen and moss.

Stellan remembered that he had read in *The Gentle Owl's Guide to Manners and Protocol* that these moss capes were the ceremonial garb for gatherings in Ambala. Hence, they came by their names—the greenowls of Ambala.

Although the yosses had just arrived, they knew that they had to wait to speak, despite their agitation over Third's capture. This would be their first effort at mustering allies. And more specifically, Stellan's first attempt in his role as frynmater—diplomat from the Great Ga'Hoole Tree. An elderly whiskered screech began. "Greetings." He nodded at them. "What brings you bears from the Whitelands so far south?" Stellan recalled that this was the peculiar name that these owls called the Nunquivik—the Whitelands, since snow and ice were rare in Ambala.

Stellan now stepped forward. "Hope and disaster bring us," he said simply.

The owl's bright yellow eyes blinked. "Disaster? Let us then hope we might help you."

"One of our own has been taken, taken—we fear—as a hostage."

"One of your own—that is terrible." His beak seemed to quiver a bit. This, Stellan had heard, was a sign that an owl had felt something deep in its gizzard. The gizzard was the most sensitive organ of any owl. All their strongest feelings and intuitions came through this muscular, thick-walled part of an owl's stomach for grinding the grit of its food.

Stellan paused. "But we also come with a message from the Great Tree."

"The Great Tree? Soren?" A look of great concern fled through the amber eyes of the owl. "The king has a message for us? It has been so long since we have heard from Soren. We feared for his health."

"Yes, sir, a message from the king. And he is fine, in good health for a creature of his years." Stellan lightly dragged one claw across the forest floor, a sign of extreme respect. Then he quickly repeated the gesture, but this time with two claws. He stepped forward and dragged the second claw again. Claw dragging was part of the protocol for presenting a serious question to the greenowls.

"A subject of vital importance. Kindly proceed."

Stellan felt caught in the amber glare of the whiskered screech's gaze. He was extremely nervous. These august owls of Ambala were considered profoundly intelligent. They were venerable because of their long history and esteemed for their intellect, but they were also legendary fighters.

"Go on," an owl who'd introduced himself as Braithe said.

Stellan coughed slightly. "Sir, we are deeply appreciative of your concern for our lost friend, Third. But we originally set out with another mission. A mission authorized by the owls of the Great Tree."

"Indeed!" Braithe replied. Stellan could not tell if Braithe was surprised or not.

"Yes. We are bears of the Nunquivik, the Far Ice, or the Whitelands as you call them. We have reason to believe that the bears who control the great Ice Clock believe the great clock to be a god. To this false god, they sacrifice young cubs, very young cubs called Tick Tocks." There was a stirring among the owls. Low murmurs of shock and disbelief. Yellow and black and brown eyes blinked and flashed with horror.

"They kill their own, their own young?"

"What would make a creature do such a thing?"

"They must have licked at the bark of the Gynyakka trees," Stellan heard a great horned next to him murmur.

"There are no such trees sir in the Far Ice. There are hardly any trees." Stellan paused and went on. He certainly had all their attention. "I cannot tell you everything except this violence needs to be stopped. We fear that it could actually spread to regions beyond the clock. More sacrifices, more young creatures' blood to please this false god." There was a gasp from all the owls draped in their moss cloaks. Stellan continued. "For this reason, we four bears have been entrusted with the mission of . . . of . . . of—"

"Speak no more," Braithe interrupted. "You need allies, am I correct?"

"Yes, sir." And then Stellan's diplomatic composure seemed to dissolve in an instant. His ears were twitching nervously. "Will you brave and learned owls help us?"

Braithe was quiet for several moments. Stellan was not sure what was happening. The whiskered screech swiveled his head slowly. The dazzling light of his eyes seeming to settle on one owl at a time. It was as if some imperceptible secret message or signal were being exchanged. Then he spoke.

"Good bears of the Nunquivik," he sighed. "All tyranny needs to gain a talonhold in these kingdoms of Ga'Hoole is for creatures of good conscience to remain silent." He paused for several seconds. "You shall excuse us perhaps while we discuss?"

"Certainly, sir," Stellan replied. He could feel Jytte flinch beside him. *Patience, Jytte*, he wanted to say. *Patience.*

"Moby." Braithe nodded at a male great snowy owl. "Would you escort the bears to the Moss Dell?"

"Aye, aye, Captain."

The three yosses exchanged glances. They had never heard these words *aye, aye* or *Captain.*

"Uh," ventured Jytte. "These are new words to us."

"And your name as well," Stellan asked. "Moby? Does this have something to do with books?"

"Indeed it does," the great snowy replied as he began to lead them down a tangled path to the Moss Dell a short distance away. When they arrived, they found hummocks and shallow gullies thick with the softest and greenest moss they had ever seen or felt. Moby swept his wing lightly over a swelling mound of the moss.

"Finest moss in the world. Rabbit Ear moss we call it. So settle back, and while you rest—and you do look tired—I'll tell you how I came to be called Moby. Moby Dick, to be precise."

"What a very odd name," Jytte murmured.

"So you have been told, I expect, by the owls of the Great Tree how the greenowls of Ambala dedicate themselves to be the guardians of the written word, of books."

"Yes," Froya replied softly. Did she really want to hear about books when her brother was missing and perhaps in mortal danger? The last thing she needed to hear were the words *Once upon a time . . .*

But that was not how Moby began. *"Call me Ishmael. Some years ago—"*

"Pardon me," Froya interrupted. "I thought your name was Moby?"

"Moby Dick is the great white whale. Now, I just love this part, so let me go on, kindly." Moby resumed, *"Having little or no money in my purse, and nothing particular to interest me on shore . . ."*

Borrring! thought Jytte, but Stellan was captivated by the gently rolling cadences of this owl's voice.

"I thought I would sail about a little and see the watery part of the world. It is a way I have of driving off the spleen, and regulating the circulation. Whenever I find myself growing grim about

the mouth; whenever it is a damp, drizzly November in my soul . . ."

The bears were uncertain how long they had been listening to Moby. Stellan appeared to find the story engaging, but Jytte and Froya were fidgety and greatly relieved when a small spotted owl appeared.

"Braithe has summoned the bears. A decision has been reached."

"At last!" Jytte muttered. They returned to the circle, where the greenowls were all perched in their moss cloaks. Stellan stepped forward.

"Bears," Braithe intoned, "first of all, I want you to know that I have already dispatched a search party for your brother." He nodded at Froya, and the bear appeared to stagger a bit.

"Thank you, sir," she replied in a trembling voice.

"This is all very odd," he continued. "We think of Ambala, these woods and forests, as places of great tranquility."

Stellan looked about, taking in the strangely serene scene of these greenowls. Could such violence have transpired here, or anywhere near this place? Yet Stellan knew that neither he, nor Jytte, nor Froya, would ever be serene until Third was back. He almost felt guilty that he had been so lulled by the story of Moby.

"And secondly," Braithe sighed, "this threat from the Far Ice in the north, this monster clock, is in fact a danger for all creatures. So, yes. Yes, we shall join you. Our decision is unanimous.

Take back our tidings to the king, Soren, and tell him that we are prepared to take up arms against this enemy."

Stellan felt relief wash through him. He looked at the owls that flanked Braithe. They were a fraction of the size of the bears, and they seemed in their draping caps of moss the most unwarlike creatures in the world. And yet he knew from their studies at the Great Tree that they led the fight long ago against a tyrannical owl who came from across the Sea of Vastness and attempted to destroy the owls of Ga'Hoole. However, they seemed so different from the owls of the Great Tree. Braithe seemed to sense Stellan's thoughts.

"You are wondering about this place, I can tell. Very different from the Great Tree."

"Indeed, sir," Stellan replied softly.

"This is the very center of the Brad, as we call it," he began to explain. "The Brad was the first book from the *fragmentum* that we rescued, and I myself committed those fragments to memory. I'm a collier by trade and had plunged into a fire to rescue this book. Only fifty pages were undamaged." He paused, then resumed. "So you see, we call this the Place of Living Books. I believe Moby began to recite one of these books that we saved. It is one of the longest ones, called *Moby Dick*, about the white whale from the time of the Others.

"This place, the Brad, was named for the author of the first book that was salvaged from the fires of the Striga, the blue owl who began the burnings. We don't know what the author's full name was, for we only had scraps of the cover. But we think it was Ray Brad." He turned his gaze on an eagle who had just alighted. He nodded at the eagle and continued talking.

"This eagle, Zyrr is his name, saved the immense eagles' nest that was at the top of a nearby heartwood tree. He too was a rescuer of books, some of the great Ezylryb's writings. And Emily"—he nodded to a small owl who wore a tiny cape of moss—"she saved Emily's poems and loved them so dearly that she renamed herself Emily." Emily was a tiny pygmy owl. She looked almost exactly like Rosie back at the tree. She struck Stellan as an especially shy owl. Quite different from Rosie.

"Emily, would you care to start off with a poem for twixt time?"

"You mean for dawn, Braithe—that's what the Others like Emily called twixt time, dawn."

"Yes."

The little pygmy wilted and became even smaller.

"I'm not sure, Braithe." She spoke in a tremulous voice.

"Emily is very shy," Braithe explained. "But her voice is so lovely. Please, Emily."

She scuffed her talons against the pine needles on the ground as if trying to work up her nerve.

"All right." In two wing beats, she was perched on a taller stump than the one she had previously occupied. The glow of the fire cast a luminous pink glow on her white eyebrow feathers and the streaks of white on her belly.

I'm nobody! Who are you?
Are you nobody, too?

Then there's a pair of us—don't tell!
They'd banish us, you know.

"I think you're somebody," Stellan said softly.

"Now, bears," Braithe said. "I know you are still missing very much your friend Third. If the search party has any news, they shall send back a messenger immediately. But they have only been gone a short time."

"Third isn't just my friend," Froya said timidly. "He's my brother."

Braithe was about to tell her not to despair, when there was a flash of green in the morning light filtering down through the crown of the heartwood tree. The three bears cried out and stiffened as they saw an immense and luminous bright green snake settle on the ground. The snake deposited a fluffy little bundle on the ground. Rags staggered to her feet.

She twisted her head this way and that. Then she spied Froya and flew toward her. "I couldn't find him. I'm so sorry." She looked around again. The three bears were cowering. Their eyes were clamped on the snake.

"Oh, don't worry. Don't worry," Braithe said quickly. "These are the greensnakes of Ambala. Yes, the deadliest venom on earth, but they are our friends. Deadlier than frost vipers but good creatures. And Efyr here is one of the best."

"Ssssssooo many thankssss, Massssster Braithe."

Braithe tossed his head and chuckled. "I am not their master at all. We are friends, colleagues."

"I prefer to addresssss you asssssss masssster."

Rags had now climbed up from Froya's arms and perched on her shoulder.

"I tried so hard to find Third, and I was just resting for a moment in a tree . . . and . . . and . . ." Her voice broke. Rags began to gulp. "I . . . I . . . can't say it."

"Say what?" Braithe asked.

The green snake slithered closer to Rags and gently lifted the tip of its tail onto the owl's shoulder to comfort her.

"Should I tell them, Ragssss?"

Rags nodded. Emily swooped down and extended a protective wing over Rags's other shoulder.

The snake Efyr continued. "Ragssssss encountered her mum, Edith, who sssseemssss to be a sssssslipgizzle for the enemy. We have had a watch on her for ssssome time. To put it ssssimply, she attacked her own child. We ssssaved Ragsss just assss she was sssstriking."

Braithe's beak dropped open. "She tried to kill her own? She's a slipgizzle?"

Rags began to sob uncontrollably. "I am ashamed! My mum, a slipgizzle! I am the child of a slipgizzle. No one will ever trust me . . ."

"No! No!" Stellan almost roared. "You are the most trustworthy owl we have ever met! I heard you getting up in the middle of the night to go out and search for Third. Were you fearful when you flew out?"

Rags nodded.

"And were you fearful when your mum, Edith, attacked?"

"Of course. It was a kill spiral!"

"Don't you understand, Rags? You have courage. There cannot be courage without fear.

"If anyone here"—Stellan cast his eyes around the circle of owls—"deserves to be Guardian of Ga'Hoole, it is you, Rags."

A peculiar mist had begun to seep through the Brad as Stellan was speaking. A stillness fell upon all the creatures as they watched slightly confused, and then in the very center, quietly with no fuss, Third stepped out of the mist.

"Third!" Froya yelped, and ran into her brother's arms.

"What? Wh-wh—" stammered Jytte.

Tears began to fill Stellan's eyes. With a trembling paw, he reached out to touch Third's shoulder, as if to confirm that this was, yes, truly Third, the cub whom they had known since his birth.

It had not struck Jytte until this very moment how awful it would have been if her own brother had been seized. She had an overpowering urge to embrace both Froya and Stellan. In that moment, she realized that without Stellan she would not be whole, not whole at all but merely a half bear. Her knees suddenly felt weak. She had to crouch down on all fours to steady herself.

"It's a *scroomfyll*," Braithe said in wonder. "I have heard of this phenomenon but never . . . never experienced it." He gasped slightly. "Never seen one. Never quite believed it."

"Believe it," Third replied softly.

"The bears that carried you off tried to moon blink you in the Canyonlands?" Braithe asked.

"Indeed, sir." Third sensed that this owl, a whiskered screech, was indeed Braithe, the leader of the greenowls of Ambala. "The scrooms saved me. I'm not sure how. But now those Roguer bears are stumbling around, moon blinked themselves, I think. At least for a while their brains will be numb."

"But where did they go, the scrooms?" Froya looked about. "I need to thank them. I . . . I owe them so much. They brought you back. My brother!" Froya began to weep. He was her younger brother, and she towered over him. But she pressed him close to her. Close to her heart and she felt his heart beating against hers. He was alive. He was here, and that was all she needed.

"I think they went back to glaumora," Braithe said softly. Then he turned to Jytte. "Come along, Jytte. I'll take you to the heartwood tree, where you can tap out your message to Blythe."

≥↔↗↩↘∩
Ⴈ∀∯∯⊗≥
≥∀∈∑∯⊗≥

In the roots of the Great Ga'Hoole Tree, Blythe bent over a tablet transcribing the taps onto a piece of parchment made from scraped rodent skin. "Good, yoss!" she whispered, praising Jytte's coded message. She was using a double encryption. The strange symbols translated into the opening lines of an ancient poem of the Others.

> *that an idle king,*
> *By this still hearth, among these barren crags*
> *Match'd with an ancient wife, I mete and dole*
> *Unequal laws unto a savage race*

Blythe breathed a huge sigh of relief. The greenowls of Ambala would join them as allies. Not only that, they would have the services of their blacksmith, Gonfyl. Gonfyl was descended from a long line of distinguished Silverveil blacksmiths but had decided to go out on her own. She was one of the few female blacksmiths.

By the time Blythe rolled up the mouseskin scroll, the ink had dissolved. There was not a trace of this message left. It was all in her head. She would report to Soren immediately.

CHAPTER 20

The Residue of a Bear

Nearly a moon had passed. The world of the Nunquivik was well into the Second Seal Moon. Lago had switched her den from the one where she had witnessed the death of Taaka. A blizzard had swept in before the Dark Feathers, the huge birds that feasted on death, were done with the carcass. Lago had set out just as the first one had landed. Foxes were deeply superstitious of having the shadows of the Dark Feathers cross one's den—even if that den was deep beneath the snow surface.

Lago was now far from the kill site, and yet that smell, not the smell of death, but the other smell that was somehow so familiar, haunted her. The scent of Illya, her sister. But that made no sense, she told herself for perhaps the one thousandth time. She had never before seen the bear who carried that scent. It was definitely not the bear that Illya had begun following those long years ago.

There were several bears now out on the ice, for the sealing was good. She had attached herself to a mother with a single yearling cub. The mother was a good still-hunter, and with only one cub, which was unusual, there were plenty of scraps for Lago. But one evening when the lights of the ahalikki were burning brightly in the sky, the bears had temporarily forgotten their hunger. Instead of still-hunting, the bears had risen up to dance under the pulsing colors of the throbbing sky. It was then that Lago caught the scent again. It was crisp and clear, unsullied by any other smell—it was pure fox. And not just any fox. It was Illya. She was certain. Lago immediately forgot about following the mother bear and her cub. She had to track down this scent.

By the time the ahaliikki had faded and the first red glow of the dawn appeared on the horizon, she found the paw prints. They were like any other Nunquivik fox's in terms of their shape and size. But there was something slightly askew about how this fox prowled the sea ice. There was an odd rhythm, or pace, as if the fox was hesitant in some way. Maybe like a kit trying out the sea ice for the first time. Despite the hesitancy, there was a fierce determination. It was clear this fox had not attached herself to any particular bear. But what was it doing? After two nights of following this scent, Lago came to an ice shelf that hung out over the edge of open water. It was a big leap to the floe on the other side. But this fox must have done it or swum. Lago eyed the dark water between herself and the ice on the other side. She realized that this must be a channel. Yes, of course, she recalled it now. It led to a tickle, which was a very narrow passage that would end on a beach just north of Winston, where the Others had once lived. The two-legs. She could see that something had clawed its way up the edge of the floe. At this distance, she couldn't see if the tracks were those of a fox or not.

Lago had no inclination to get wet. It was a big gap to jump, but she had to try. She circled around to get some distance, and then running full out, she leaped, arcing high into the night, clearing the edge of the floe easily. Apparently, this fox had decided to swim. Lago went back and peered at where the fox had clawed its way out of the sea. The scent, though slightly diluted from the salt water, was still strong.

This particular floe carried a strange ice formation that the foxes called ice stars, for it appeared like a star that had fallen from the sky. They only emerged from the floes when the air was extremely cold and dry, colder than the water. Water vapor from the sea collects, then becomes crystalized and drops onto the floe, creating spiky threads of ice that radiate from a core.

Nunquivik foxes were very light. Not only that but they were nimble and experts in treading softly. If Lago could climb this ice star, she would have a terrific vantage point to scan the sweeping icescape. Delicately, she lifted a paw and tested an ice spike. She gave a small jump, extended a front paw to a higher spike as her hind paw rested on the lower one. She was almost at the top and pleased to see that several of the spikes had woven together to provide a small platform. She tucked her tail beneath her and had a perfect perspective. Her eyes swept the icescape. She was on a floe, but there were several others floating nearby in the calm waters of this channel. She could see where the channel narrowed into the tickle that flowed darkly between the edges of two ice sheets.

The diminishing red glow that signaled the dawn was already fading. A new twilight was coming and then the long, long night of this seal moon. A shadow spread across the ice sheet. It was that of a fox. Was it the fox of the familiar scent? Could it be? She was sprinting now, obviously on the track of a lemming, but her tail movements were awkward. It was as if she were not quite accustomed to using her tail for balance. She had the Northing. It was obvious. And she was about to leap. She sprang into the air and tried to rudder her tail to stabilize herself. But the tail hung loosely between her legs, as if she didn't know what to do with it. *You idiot!* Lago wanted to scream. But she couldn't. It was, after all, her sister, Illya! She was the shape of a fox. She tracked like a fox, but it was as if the residue of a bear dragged through her. "So it's true," Lago murmured to herself. And she felt that her heart might break. Her sister had in fact made a fanciful den story about shape-shifters come to life. It was no fantasy but a dreadful reality. She had bartered her true nature for this folly! *Why?* Lago wondered with disgust.

"Well," muttered Illya as she came up from her dive, "I certainly made a mess of that!"

"Indeed, you did, sister," Lago said, stepping out of the shadows.

Illya gasped, then went rigid. She appeared as spiky as the ice star, and in fact her pelt hung with icicles, for she had swum that gap. Then she began shaking. The icicles of her fur began to rattle eerily in the darkening night.

"What? How? How . . ."

"You need to melt," Lago said matter-of-factly. "Seriously, you need to melt." She approached Illya and, with her warm tongue, began to groom her, the way they used to groom each other when they were young. But, of course, back in those days, neither of them had been stupid enough to try to swim on a night like this. Their fur had never frozen.

Illya closed her eyes as her sister's warm breath and tongue licked away the icicles.

"Now give a good shake," Lago ordered. And like an obedient kit, Illya shook herself. There was the rattle of the last remaining icicles. It was as if Illya and her younger sister had exchanged places. Lago was now the one ordering her about.

When she had melted completely, she stood in front of Lago and blinked several times, her golden eyes like winking stars. "So how did you find me? How did you know?"

"Believe me, it wasn't easy. I picked up your scent on another bear."

"What other bear?"

"I believe her name was Svenna."

"Svenna!" The very sound of the name cut her to the quick.

"Was she a bad bear?"

Illya shook her head wearily. "Oh, no. Never. She was the best bear at the Ice Clock. The only good bear. "

"You were at the Ice Clock?"

Illya nodded and seemed to shrink in shame. "But I went for a good reason."

"What possible good reason could you have to go to that cursed place with those evil bears?"

"To stop the clock," Illya replied quietly.

Lago shook her head in confusion. "You went as a bear, didn't you?"

"How did you know?"

"Because you walk, you track, you leap as no fox I've ever seen."

"It's hard getting back into one's own skin."

"So it was all true—the Ki-hi-ru stories?"

Illya nodded.

"But why? Why did you ever do this?"

"For love," Illya answered simply. And tipped her head toward the signpost. "Winston Pop. 302," she read the sign aloud.

"You can read, Illya?" Lago said softly.

"Oh, Lago, you would be surprised what I can do."

"For the love of reading you went?" Lago was shaking her head in disbelief.

"Not exactly for the love of reading, but love of a bear." She gave a small cough as if she were slightly embarrassed that she had even said the word *love*. "But I sure made a mess of trying to catch that lemming, didn't I?"

Lago nodded, then said softly, "Don't worry. I'll catch some." She turned to go off. "Now watch me do it."

In a short time, she was back with three plump lemmings.

"Thank you, Lago." Illya looked down at the lemmings hungrily. "It's been so long . . . since . . ." She didn't finish. Her voice just trailed off.

"What happened, Illya?"

Illya felt a little shiver of not cold but delight. Her name! She could have her true name back! "It's a long story." She looked up at Lago, her eyes sparkling with tears. "But it feels so good to hear my true name spoken out loud."

"What other name do you have?"

"Galilya."

"What kind of name is that?"

"A bear name. As I say, it's a long story. And it began with love."

"So this bear you loved, Uluk Uluk, was he the one you began following in my third season—the sad bear, we called him?"

"Yes, but he wasn't sad when I . . . I . . ."

"Changed, transformed?" Lago asked.

Again, Illya nodded and cast her eyes down as if she were profoundly ashamed.

Lago's heart went out to her. "But you did it for love, Illya."

"Yes, I denied my own nature, my very being for love."

"Were you happy with him?" Lago took a step closer to her sister and peered into her eyes, turning her head ever so slightly this way and that, as if trying to reach into her sister's brain. How could this have happened? How could she have fallen in love with a creature so different from her own true self?

"Oh yes. He taught me so much. How to read. He taught me the way of the timepieces and the great Ice Clock." Illya sighed and shook her head. It was so difficult to explain.

"Go on," Lago said gently, and nuzzled the withers on her sister's neck to encourage her. She knew this was hard for Illya. It had to be. Illya had discarded her own identity as if it had meant nothing. And now she radiated shame. Lago knew she had to listen patiently.

"And he told me the danger the clock threatened. He himself had been a high-ranking member of the Gilraan, the ministry, the highest order of authority at the Ice Clock, before he was suspected of spying and was exiled, kicked out." She paused for a long time. "That's when I first met him, after he was kicked out." She sighed. "And then he kicked me out."

"Why?"

"He was away, and I just briefly shifted back to my true shape. And when he came into . . . into the containment facility . . ." She tipped her head a bit to the east.

"The what?"

"It's this place, where we lived. Hard to explain. But he was furious. He called me all sorts of horrible names. I, of course, left."

"Why didn't you come home? Were you too ashamed?"

"Not enough! I decided even if he no longer loved me, even if he hated me, I would travel to the Ice Clock as a bear and attempt to carry out his plan for stopping the clock. He had taught me everything he knew about clockmaking. He said

I would have been admitted in the time of the Others to the Society of Supreme Clockmakers in Geneva. Yes, that's how good he thought I was." Illya's eyes grew shimmery as she thought back to those moments in her life with Uluk Uluk. "And so, even though he loathed me, I wanted to show him what I could do. And if I did it, I thought he might take me back."

A coldness crept through Lago. She could not quite believe what she was hearing. "You want to go back to him now?"

"Not to be loved. To go in my own skin and tell him what I have learned. You see, Uluk Uluk thought we could do it without the key. But we can't. I know what the Grand Patek is planning. A countdown has begun. At a certain moment, the bungvik will break and . . . and . . . and the rest of the world will wash away . . . drowned. My friend Udo and I figured this out. We also tried to slow the clock. But it must be stopped. With the key. The key, it is now rumored, is in the paws, rather the talons, of owls. We need the owls of Ga'Hoole, and we also need a force, an army of rebel bears. They are out there, I know it. But Uluk Uluk will know how to gather them. He is old, decrepit, but he is a legend and will be listened to, despite his age. He could lead."

Lago's fur bristled. She stood erect. "I'll go with you."

"You don't need to."

"I know that, but this bear is going to see two foxes standing in front of him. Proudly standing in front of him!" she added.

Beyond the Beyond

CHAPTER 21

In a Strange Land

The four yosses were together again. And it felt right and good. The terrible rent that had been left when those Roguers had torn Third from them had been mended. They felt almost stronger than they had before. And not only that but Rags had decided to accompany them. She had become an expert flyer. "You need me," she announced just as they were setting out. "I can be your scout."

"But I thought you wanted to be with your own kind."

"You're my kind in more ways than you might think."

Stellan stopped and peered with delight at the young spotted owl. "Actually, Rags, you are our ally. You are the very first ally of this allied force that Soren charged us to gather."

"I think I am first your friend, and you all are mine. Call it whatever name you like!" And they continued winding their way across a broad swath of Ga'Hoole. From Ambala, they had traveled to across the Barrens, taking the shortest route over the narrowest part that bordered Silverveil. There they had met with a lovely snowy owl, a female called Tula who presided over the owls of that forest. "We have one of the best units of Frost Beaks in all the kingdoms, trained in the Northern Kingdoms after the last great war."

"That would be the War of the Ember, would it not?" Stellan inquired.

Jytte looked at her brother. He had become the consummate diplomat. He had the perfect temperament. She did not! She readily admitted this to herself. Patience and reflection were not part of her nature.

But Stellan, despite this success, was still anxious. Now they were heading into the territory of the Beyond. A bitter cold wind scraped across the barren landscape. What would these wolves be like? They had never met a wolf before. There were not many in the Nunquivik. Wolves there were sometimes known to attack very young cubs. That was why their mother had never left them unguarded in the den when they were newborn. The wolves hunted in packs, and this idea was truly peculiar to the minds of bears, who always hunted alone. Only so many bears could sit by an ice hole waiting for a seal to poke its nose up.

These wolves of the Beyond were said to be very different from any of the wolves in the Nunquivik. The wolf packs that they lived in were each part of a clan. The yosses had been required to learn all the clans' names before they left. Each clan had a leader, and there were elaborate customs and rules that governed every aspect of their lives. From birth until death. A malformed pup, called a *malcadh*, was always cast out of the clan, left to die or be devoured by a predator. If, however, it survived, it became a gnaw wolf, the lowest-ranking wolf in the clan. The duty of a malcadh was to carve the bones of prey into symbols and designs that recorded the clan history. Some of these gnaw wolves could rise, however, and serve at the Ring of the Sacred Volcanoes. Malcadh was just one of the peculiar words of the wolf language. What Stellan was seeking now was *parlagh*, a conference with a clan chieftain.

This wolf world of the Beyond was so complicated that it almost defied any creature from the outside to ever understand it. They held within them a distance that defied breaching.

As they entered the Beyond, Third noticed how the trees were quickly thinning out, and how they were not only fewer but much smaller. It was as if these could not grow against the continuous harsh onslaught of the winds. They reminded Third of crooked old animals fighting against the overwhelming powers of nature. He'd seen bears like those out on the sea ice in the Nunquivik. They were called in old Krakish *Vlimyk vintur*, which translated to last winter hunters. They looked beaten and shriveled and most likely they would not live until the next winter.

The scouring winds of the Beyond were nothing for these four young bears. However, Stellan, as the frynmater, the diplomat, felt caught in a whirlwind of facts, particulars, and instructions about the culture of this strange land. First, there were all the new words that only wolves used—words like *gaddernock*, which was the complete and sacred laws, codes, and traditions of the wolves of the Beyond. They must not transgress any of those. And then there was a myriad of words and rules pertaining to the Ring of Sacred Volcanoes, from which the collier owls came during certain seasons of eruption to harvest the coals. The Fengo was the chieftain of the Ring of Sacred Volcanoes. And there were the very precise rules of protocol that governed how a creature approached a pack, the pack leader, and the clan leader. There had been so much to learn and so much to remember.

"I see Beezar!" Jytte called out, and stopped, rising up on her hind legs to point to the fighting bear constellation. In the wolf world, this constellation was called the Blind Wolf.

"I think we're getting close to the MacDuff territory," Froya said. It was as if the map she had studied for those long hours was now emblazoned on her brain as bright as this starlit wind-scoured night. She looked up and saw that Rags's flight was a bit errant in these adverse winds. *She's tired*, Froya thought.

"Rags, come down. Settle on my shoulder. These winds are too stiff for you."

"No, they aren't." It had to be nearly impossible for her, Froya thought. She was half the weight of one of her paws.

"Yes, come on!" Jytte called. "We've traveled a fair distance. We're all hungry. We all need to eat something."

"Actually . . ." Rags emitted a swooping hoot of excitement. "It's . . . it's a caribou!"

"But how can that be?" Froya exclaimed. "It's not the Caribou Moon now. The Caribou Moon is an autumn moon."

Jytte gave Froya a withering glance. "You can be a dead caribou in any moon." Sometimes, Froya could be slightly annoying. She was quite literal and a stickler for facts.

"Dead and no vultures," Froya added.

Ahead, they saw Rags swooped down on what at first they thought was a snow-covered rock, but it was the rump of the caribou. When they arrived, Rags flew and perched on the animal's antlers. "I'm not sure how long ago it was killed, but there is plenty left for us. Well, probably not me. One needs fangs for this job."

"Don't worry," Stellan said. "I'll tear a hunk off for you. After all, you spotted it. Therefore you should get the first bite. Don't the wolves have a lot of rules about who gets to eat first after a kill?"

"Yes, but I didn't kill it."

"You found it." And with that Stellan approached the neck of the creature, where there was an open wound, and tore some flesh. "I might have to shred that up for you a bit."

"Thank you, Stellan," Rags replied.

After Rags had her first bite, the rest began to tear greedily at the carcass. A rising moon, large and luminous as a silvery bubble, wobbled on the horizon. They hardly noticed when a strange shadow began to slide over the carcass they were feasting on. But then, all at once, they froze. A dread filled Froya. She turned around.

A magnificent wolf stood in complete silence. Unlike other wolves they had learned about, this wolf's eyes were not really green but a deep, almost midnight blue. Its pelt was gilded in frost and moonlight. The bears felt themselves enveloped in a thick silence, but finally, Stellan fell to his knees and began crawling toward the wolf. This was the first of the submission postures he had read about in *The Gentle Owl's Guide to Manners and Protocol*. Tucking his tail was difficult as it was so short. As he drew closer, he began to roll onto his back and lift his paws as if to scratch at the stars.

"Not necessary," the wolf barked. "First submission posture is adequate. No need to advance to second."

Jytte turned her head to look at Stellan. He knew exactly what she was thinking. *Submission? Really? Looks like groveling to me.* But such were the ways of the wolves.

"My name is Alasdair. I am a scout for the MacDuncan clan." She paused and cast her eyes on Rags. "The she-winds are blowing. You tried, little owl. You have good marrow." The wolf spoke in a beautiful lilting cadence, and when she said the word *marrow*, it almost seemed to trill in the frosty air.

The notion was slightly alarming, and before Rags could mind her beak, she blurted out, "Actually, truth be told, I have no marrow. My bones are hollow."

"It doesn't matter. The owls might say you have a bit of Ga in ye." She turned to the other wolves and spoke. "Where do you go? What do you seek?"

Stellan stepped forward. "We seek parlagh with the chieftain of your clan."

"You speak our language well, bear. Now follow me. I'll take you to the gadderheal of the MacDuncan clan." The swooping cadences of her voice were like music.

"MacDuncan clan!" Stellan exclaimed. "I thought we were close to the MacNab clan." Otulissa had recommended going to the MacNab clan first. She had told them that the MacNabs had risen in the last few years to become one of the most influential clans. If one could convince the MacNabs to join the alliance, it would make it easier with the other five clans.

"Ah, no, you see, in the time of Faolan"—upon uttering this name, the wolf Alasdair dropped to one knee, then sprang up again—"when the Wolf of all Wolves left, it was because of an earthquake. Many left with him and went across the ice bridge in the far west. It has only been in recent years that many of those who left have returned. The clan borders were redrawn. Alas, same old squabbles."

"Squabbles?" Third asked. Third knew that the wolves were very territorial. They did not tolerate trespassers. Although the bears had studied the maps, apparently those maps didn't exactly seem to work now, not since the great earthquake of some twenty years before. Too bad, Third thought, that they didn't have more up-to-date maps. They would have to carefully pick their routes and try to figure out whose territory they were crossing. Seeing as both Third and Froya were the navigators, the responsibility was on them. It was rather like moving blind through an unknown landscape during a blizzard.

"Never mind. Follow me." The beautiful wolf Alasdair began to trot off. Then she turned and called back, "And in the gadderheal when meeting the chieftain, you can carry out the complete range of submission postures for visiting non-wolf species." She paused. "He is very formal, Chieftain MacDuncan. More so than other chieftains."

Stellan and the other three bears exchanged nervous glances. Otulissa had seemed to think it was important that they ease into the Beyond. She knew their customs would be quite foreign to the bears and for this reason as well felt they should first be introduced to the MacNabs. *Very formal. What if we make a mistake?* Jytte, Third, and Froya were all thinking the same thing. Otulissa had said that the wolves were vital to any success if there was war. They were superb fighters, efficient, strategic, and relentless on the battlefield.

Alasdair sensed the bears' anxiety. She could try to put them at their ease, but it would do no good. She couldn't help but recall a conversation she had overheard just the day before between Duncan MacDuncan and his mate. The chieftain always seemed to be yearning for something bigger, grander, more important. That was the reason for all the quarrels with the neighboring clans concerning the territorial boundaries. For some reason, the chieftain felt he deserved that land. Alasdair had been made scout because she had an extraordinary sense of smell and could detect the slightest infringement of another clan member on the MacDuncan hunting grounds. She had overheard a peculiar conversation once when the chieftain was talking to his mate, Liathe.

"You know, my dear, if we were owls . . . ," he was saying.

"Duncan, whatever are you talking about . . . if we were owls?"

"All I am saying is that if we were I'd be a king and you'd be a queen."

"Oh, what does that matter, Duncan? You're a chieftain. Is that not enough?"

Alasdair was struck by the oddness of this conversation—a wolf wanting to be an owl? Yet the chieftain never mentioned wings or flying. That was the only advantage that Alasdair could think of for becoming an owl. She wondered if any other creatures longed to slip the cloak or pelt of their species and become another. These bears of the north appeared content in their own skin. The four young bears seemed like good creatures to her. Although she was unsure why they wanted to meet with the chieftain, they had obviously crossed over from Ga'Hoole. The scent of the Great Tree was on them. She would lead them to the gadderheal and try to give them some advice that might help them during their parlagh with the chieftain.

She turned to Stellan. "Now, try not to be nervous. You did that first submission posture very well when we met."

They followed the wolf Alasdair for several leagues, passing perhaps two or three wolf packs of the MacDuncan territory. Their pelts ranged in color from gray to reddish and tan. A few were pure white. There was a grace to their light, absolutely soundless gait. Prey would never hear them coming. It was their silence that was slightly eerie. They might as well be walking on air, Froya thought. There was something almost ghostly about them, especially now, as a heavy snow began to fall, slanting against the harsh wind. The figures of the wolves appeared like silhouettes behind the scrim of the growing blizzard. They were curious but kept their distance. One might emerge from a pack cave and stare at them rather indifferently, then return to its cave. The first time this happened, Stellan was unsure of the protocol.

"Do we need to do the submission greeting for the packs, Alasdair?"

"No, you're with me, and we're just passing through on our way to the gadderheal."

"So the chieftain is Duncan MacDuncan, right?"

"Yes, that has always been the custom of any chieftain in a clan. They take as their first name the last part of the clan name—like Nab MacNab or Duff MacDuff—we just passed through a slice of the MacDuff territory over there."

"What about the MacHeaths?" Jytte asked.

Stellan stopped in his tracks. *How could she mention the MacHeaths?* They were the most treacherous clan in the Beyond.

Alasdair gave a low growl and swung around, lowering her head. Her eyes cast a shimmering blue light on Jytte.

"We don't speak of them. They returned, unfortunately, after the Great Leaving to the Distant Blue. We had hoped they had perished on the ice bridge but apparently not."

Jytte felt a surge of humiliation. She should have known better. She'd forgotten what Otulissa had told them about the complicated relations between clans. But the MacHeaths were shunned by every clan in the Beyond. Even outclanners who belonged to no clan shunned the MacHeaths. The clan that interested Jytte the most, however, was the MacNamara clan, the only clan led by a female—the Namara. This clan lived on the most distant outreaches of the Beyond.

A howl pierced the air and the cubs all turned their heads at once. It was a rather lovely sound, Stellan thought. The howling seemed to create a peculiar piping music that swept across the vastness of this land.

"What is that?" Stellan asked.

"We are passing the territory of the River Pack of the MacDuncan clan. That's Greer da Greer, the skreeleen, the howler, the storyteller of the pack. We can rest here a moment and listen. Her mother was one of the greatest howlers in the Beyond. Also named Greer. That's what her name means, Greer daughter of Greer."

They paused.

"Oh, dear, look at that poor little wolf!" Third said. "She looks so hungry and raggedy."

"Gnaw wolf," Alasdair replied matter-of-factly.

"Oh," Third said, and clamped his mouth shut. They had been told about gnaw wolves, the lowest-ranking pack members. They ate last, slept far from the warmth of a pack den, and endured endless abuse until they could prove themselves as expert gnawers of bone and incise precise designs that might eventually qualify them to become wolves at the Watch of the Ring of Sacred Volcanoes.

"But what is the story the skreeleen is howling?" Froya asked.

"Oh . . ." Alasdair almost gasped. Stellan immediately detected a sadness, a silent weeping in the wolf's mind. "It's telling the story of an outcast wolf, a peculiar wolf that some thought was a Sark, a witch. They called her the Sark of the Slough, for she lived in a marshy region, in a cavern. She toyed with fire." Alasdair paused and then said darkly, "She disturbed the order."

Froya was attentive. In all their preparation at the Great Tree with Otulissa, she had never told them about any witch, any creature called the Sark of the Slough.

"Was this just a legend?" Froya asked.

"Some would like to think. But no!" Alasdair said emphatically. "She was not a legend."

And in that moment, Stellan knew that the Sark of the Slough was indeed not a legend and not a witch, but someone very dear to Alasdair. This was what had made her so sad. This was the deep secret that lived within this beautiful wolf, a secret that Alasdair herself might have sensed but not yet realized as true.

CHAPTER 22

The Gadderheal

The gadderheal was perfectly concealed and from a distance appeared like a pile of gnarled logs or tree stumps beneath an overhang of a large rock. To enter, the bears had to crawl down a slope for a fair distance. Their heads often scraped the ceiling. But then the space opened up, and on an elevated ledge covered with animal skins, Duncan MacDuncan sat tall. His muzzle twist was neatly braided and hung down beneath his chin. Only clan chiefs and members of the Watch at the Sacred Ring of Volcanoes were permitted to braid their fur in this manner. One paw was placed on a long bone from an animal that stood much taller than a wolf. The bone was known as the Bone of Truth. Each clan leader had one that had been gnawed by a gnaw wolf of their clan.

Otulissa had told them about the central importance of gnawed, incised bones in this world of wolves. But what a strange world this was, thought Stellan. Otulissa and others at the Great Tree had described the Beyond as being "of Ga'Hoole" but not "in Ga'Hoole." A subtle difference that the bears did not grasp at the time but were beginning to understand now. The hierarchical society of the wolves with their elaborate caste system, or rather pack order, and reserved manners set them apart from any other species the bears had ever encountered. Their lives were layered with elaborate rituals for hunting, gnawing bones, eating their kill. And now, as Stellan gazed about, he saw several wolves that he judged to be clan elders wearing elaborate headdresses and necklaces made from the small bones of perhaps rabbits or rodents. There were only two sounds in the cave—that of the sizzling coals in the center, where a small fire burned, and then the peculiar clicking of the bone headdresses when a wolf might tip its head this way or that.

The bears immediately commenced with the submission postures. Stellan accidentally rolled on top of Jytte, but she suppressed a growl. *DO NOT GROWL!* Otulissa had warned them. There were other rules they must follow. They were not to speak until spoken to. Although a chieftain might approach them to sniff or touch, as is customary between many animals on first meeting, such conduct is strictly forbidden for the visiting creature. When leaving the presence of the chieftain, one was supposed to back away, but never, *never* turn their hindquarters to the chieftain.

The initial submission gestures had now been completed. The chieftain gave a short bark. "You may rise to a crouching posture now . . . no more." The bears all nodded that they understood. "Whom among you shall speak?"

"I shall speak, Honorable Chieftain," Stellan replied. He had been told by Otulissa that after addressing the chieftain once by his proper title he could call him sir.

"Are you the leader of this pack?"

"We have no leaders, sir," Stellan replied.

"No leader! How peculiar."

How peculiar—I'll tell you who's peculiar, Jytte thought. Relief swept through Stellan that she had not blurted that out.

"We have come, sir, at the request of Soren, the—"

"I know who Soren is," snapped Duncan MacDuncan.

"—to request that you join and rise up against these evil bears of the far north in the Nunquivik who threaten all of Ga'Hoole with their worship of this hideous clock. We ask you as faithful servants of truth and justice. We come to the Beyond, this land of valor, to ask that you join us against these depraved bears."

Third's eye filled with tears as he listened to Stellan's eloquent pleas. How could Duncan MacDuncan not be moved? Jytte was thinking the same as well. How could the chieftain not be moved?

But Stellan peered hard as he riddled the chieftain's mind and knew he had not been moved in the least. Yet Duncan MacDuncan replied in a respectful, gentle voice.

"You know, bears, that we have only recently returned to this land after the great upheavals wreaked upon us by a cataclysmic earthquake from long before you were born. Now, just two generations past in the time of my great-great-grandfather Chieftain Duncan MacDuncan, the land was broken. The Ring of Sacred Volcanoes flattened. Yet, praise Lupus, they have come back. There was famine—terrible famine as well. We few who managed to finally return have devoted all our energies to rebuilding this, our homeland. We returned against all odds and perilous conditions across the ice bridge from the Distant Blue. It was a costly and risky effort, and now that we are back, we must preserve our energies and not squander them." *Tight paws*, Stellan thought. "Therefore, I cannot indulge the demands of an owl king, or princeling bears."

All four bears blinked.

Stellan tried to imagine why the chieftains would ever think they were royal. The bears had never in all their history had kings or queens, princesses or princes. And this word *princeling* seemed to Stellan somehow demeaning, actually humiliating. As if the bears were attempting to be something they were not. Fake royalty. How should he answer him? He, after all, was the frynmater, but this wolf did not inspire friendliness.

After a pause, Stellan spoke up. "Honorable chieftain, this is not a war of chieftains or princes, of dynasties or territorial ambition. It is a war of creatures, good creatures. There are vast numbers, not only in the Beyond the Beyond, but in every land of Ga'Hoole, who will render faithful service in this war, but whose names will never be known, whose deeds will never be recorded. This is a War of the Unknown Warriors."

The chieftain, Duncan MacDuncan, appeared to be somewhat taken aback. But he shook the Bone of Truth. "I take no offense at these impertinent remarks. Convey my salutations to your king, Soren. You are dismissed."

Impertinent, Jytte thought. *How could this wolf call her brother impertinent?* This did not bode well. To be called insolent by the chieftain of the MacDuncans, which Otulissa had called the Clan of Clans, was bad. Jytte felt as if their mission was failing before it even started. The wolves were key to any alliance. The owls could control the airspace, but the wolves were vital to the land.

The bears crouched low again and began to back out of the gadderheal as they had been instructed. But Stellan could not resist one last remark. "Honorable chieftain, Soren prefers not to be addressed or referred to as a king, though he is one of the most honorable, I can imagine." Stellan gave a curious inflection to the word *honorable.* "Though indeed he is a king, he wears no crown." *He needs none of the raiments of a king or a chieftain,* Stellan thought. And then he recalled Rosie's words about Soren when they first came to the Great Ga'Hoole Tree. *Although Soren is king, and the wisest king this tree has ever had, he wears that title lightly. He is serious about his duty, but he doesn't think that being called a king requires more than just a word, a title, or a name. You'll see when you meet him. He is a rare owl like no other you've ever met.*

Outside the gadderheal, Alasdair was waiting for them.

"And how did it go?" she asked.

"Not well," Jytte replied. "We got nothing. He called us impertinent!"

Third gave a soft snarl. "He spoke down to us. As if we were—were dirt!" Third spat out the word. The other three bears were in fact shocked. Third rarely displayed such contempt.

The wolf sighed. "I was afraid of that."

"Why?" Stellan asked. His first attempt in the Beyond as a frynmater had failed miserably. He tried to quell a desperate feeling that was taking hold of him deep in his gut. It seemed as if he could almost hear that fiendish Ice Clock ticking away. The notched escapement wheel with its jagged teeth devouring the small cubs.

"This clan tends to be stingy. We don't feel a deep connection to the rest of Ga'Hoole, especially since our return from the Distant Blue. We were always isolated creatures and now even more so." Stellan was studying Alasdair hard. There was something else that was troubling her. And it wasn't just the chieftain's stinginess. What could it be? She was such a good creature. He knew it. Was she in some way at odds with this clan, or was it just the chieftain? Alasdair had cautioned them about the chieftain. Alasdair's mind was a difficult one to riddle. But he sensed a peculiar grief. There almost seemed to be a hole in her mind, or was it her spirit. Something that suggested that she did not even know the source of her own despair. He looked into her beautiful blue eyes and saw only desolation. But how could she be desolate? She lived in this clan with twenty or more other wolves. He remembered now he had sensed this before, when they had passed River Pack of the MacDuncan clan and heard the mournful voice of the storyteller, skreeleen Greer da Greer. Suddenly, Stellan felt very fearful for her.

Was he the only one who felt this? It would occupy him for the next days as they made their way to the MacNab clan. He followed right behind Alasdair, who was to take them to the border of the MacNab territory, where another scout would pick them up. All while he walked behind her, he tried to riddle her mind, but the beautiful wolf was unriddlable. Her mind was locked and would suffer no trespassers.

CHAPTER 23

Third Dreamwalks

Stellan was wrapped in a fog of despondency. Depressing thoughts chased though his mind. He was the frynmater, and yet he had failed miserably with Duncan MacDuncan. What if he failed with the MacNab chieftain and then the MacAngus chieftain and the MacDuffs? And he sensed that the other yosses were thinking the same thing. Would Third have made a better frynmater? He, after all, was the smallest of the four of them. That might have worked to his advantage. Stellan regretted his size, as perhaps being the largest he appeared threatening in some way? Maybe he just wasn't the right bear for this task.

At the border, they bid Alasdair good-bye. She tipped her head to the sky and the scudding clouds as a beautiful sound unfurled from her throat. She was calling the next scout. Within seconds, another howl floated back to them.

She turned to Stellan. "Cinead will meet you in a quarter of a league."

"And we'll recognize him?" Third asked.

"Oh yes, he's a red wolf, a very red wolf—that's what his name means—Cinead, born of fire."

This was intriguing to all the bears. "I don't think," Froya said, "I've ever met a creature with red fur. This will be interesting."

And it was. A quarter league ahead, just as Alasdair had said, they saw in the swirling snow what looked like pale fire in the distance. As they came closer and the snow ceased, it was as if they were in fact approaching red flames. But it was a wolf with an extremely luxuriant pelt that streamed out like licks of fire.

Stellan stepped forward. He was transfixed by this creature. He nodded. "Cinead?"

"Indeed," the wolf replied.

"We are here."

"Yes, I know. To gnaw words with the chieftain, Nab MacNab."

"Yes, to . . ." Stellan hesitated. ". . . gnaw words with the chieftain." He had not heard this expression before. There was nothing in *The Gentle Owl's Guide to Manners and Protocol* about gnawing words. But gnawing bones was an art form for the wolves and the word *gnaw*, Stellan reasoned, might be used for other things.

They followed Cinead for quite a distance, keeping their eyes on his flaming pelt.

"No way we can lose this wolf," Jytte whispered to Third, who trotted beside her in the deepening snow.

"Not unless he gets buried out here. This snow's coming down pretty hard."

But a short time later, they were at the MacNab gadderheal and on their bellies sliding down the entrance.

Nab MacNab was less intimidating than Duncan MacDuncan. He seemed more at ease than Duncan MacDuncan and listened carefully. Stellan had presented the request with all due formality. So far, the chieftain had not said anything about princelings but had asked some intelligent questions about the threat of the Ice Clock.

"And you say, this Ice Clock is looked upon as a divinity?"

"Indeed, sir," Stellan replied. He desperately wished he could shrink himself a bit. Appear a little more vulnerable, even perhaps a little desperate. Who was he kidding? He was desperate.

"And this bear, the Grand Patek, I believe I have heard of him and certainly not good things. Word has begun to trickle down from the Far Ice about him. But he is like . . . like what did you call him?"

"A priest."

"An unusual word."

"I believe it is a word from the time of the Others. Or also the word 'minister' has been used. And there is a ministry of

Timekeeper bears at the Ice Clock. They are called the Gilraan."

"This god clock demands a sacrifice of young creatures, and you feel the worshippers of this clock might seek fresh blood here in our lands?"

"Absolutely, sir."

"Give me a moment to reflect." He bent his head toward his counselors, and they began to whisper. The click of the bone ornaments peppered the air.

I cannot fail! I just can't. If I fail here . . . Jytte reached out her paw to give him a gentle pat. It was as if his younger sister had indeed riddled his thoughts. He cast a glance toward her. Her eyes brimmed with sympathy. *I'm here, Stellan. Right beside you, now and forever!* Her unspoken words came through with complete clarity.

The bears continued to wait tensely for a response. Nab MacNab was a gray wolf and finally he leaned forward.

"And you say that Tula, the snowy owl of Silverveil, has promised to send in her Frost Beak unit?"

"Indeed, sir," Stellan replied. "As well as the service of the Silverveil blacksmith Gwynn."

Nab MacNab's eyebrow lifted. "Impressive," he said quietly. There was a long pause. "And have you considered coals?"

"Coals?" Stellan asked, glancing at the fire.

"Not those. Those are simple coals. Coals to keep us warm. Coals to illuminate the bones while the gnaw wolves carve their designs. I am speaking of *bonk* coals."

Something stirred somewhere in each one of the bear's memories. There had been so much to learn at the Great Tree. They now dimly recollected a short lecture about bonk coals, delivered by a ruddy-feathered great horned, Buster, grandson of Bubo, the Great Tree's most famous blacksmith. They had only spent one short evening after tween time visiting his forge. But now they remembered that bonk coals were high energy, the strongest coals that could be harvested from forest fires.

Nab MacNab continued. "Yes, I see a glimmer in your eyes. You do remember how powerful bonk coals can be!"

"Yes, sir, now we do. The powerful coals from forest fires," Stellan said, barely able to contain his excitement.

"And you do not recall that the most powerful of the bonks can be harvested from the Ring of Sacred Volcanoes."

"Oh yes!" Jytte now said excitedly. "Honorable Chieftain," she added quickly, as this was the first time she had addressed Nab MacNab. "We have heard this, but we are forbidden to enter the ring."

"Not if you have a guide." He fixed Jytte in his green gaze. "Now, listen to me, bears of the Nunquivik. We wolves of the Beyond are in a fragile condition since the devastation of our lands. Our return from the Distant Blue was filled with hardship. When we returned, we were weak—weak and hungry. Every moon is a hunger moon for us now." *Oh no*, thought Froya. *This is going the way it went with Duncan MacDuncan.* "But I will give you two things." Again, the wolf paused. "First, I shall provide you with a guide to the Ring of Sacred Volcanoes. I shall also personally send a message to Soren that his best colliers should come with their buckets to harvest coals. For many bonk coals will be needed."

Jytte was suddenly nervous. She raised a paw. Nab MacNab nodded at her.

"Sir, we are profoundly grateful for this generous offer. It is so kind. But to send a message to Soren could be exceedingly dangerous."

"Of course, young'un, you are completely correct. I should have thought of that. Unfortunately, slipgizzles are not unknown in the Beyond. I trust you have a secure way to transmit this message. So I'll leave that to you." He again paused. "And I shall promise the owls one more service."

"Service?" Third asked.

"Yes, a service. Tell the honorable owls of the Great Tree that I shall send a *slink melf*."

"A what?" Stellan asked.

"A slink melf is a special commando team of wolves, an assassination squad to bring down any enemy who endangers a clan. In this coming war, a slink melf could be very useful in any covert operations."

The bears were completely astonished. Truly overwhelmed by the grace and generosity of this chieftain, Stellan was not simply amazed but now wondered why Duncan MacDuncan seemed to have been so dismissive. He had never even asked a single question, whereas Nab MacNab had asked so many. Perhaps he should have tried harder to explain the imminent danger to Duncan MacDuncan.

As soon as they were out of the territory of the chieftain's pack, Jytte began scanning the landscape for the special rocks that Blythe had told her about, *spryss* rocks, or whisper rocks. That had excellent sound-transmitting potential. *You tap on a spryss rock and your message comes through clear as a bell!* Blythe had said.

The bears did not have to go far to find one. They all watched as Jytte crouched over the dark gray rock that was embedded with red veins. She began tapping with her two claws simultaneously. She was fast. Her claws flashed over the stone. Her brother, Froya, and Third watched her in amazement. Hopefully there would be a response soon. When Blythe was not in the roots, there was always another owl there if a message came through, who would then fly out and find Blythe to come back.

The bears waited tensely for a response. Jytte kept her ear pressed to the rock. A tap came through. *Again!* was the simple command. She must send the coded message once again, as Blythe was now back at her station. It would take a while, since Jytte had once more used the double-encryption method. The other bears watched, transfixed. Stellan could not help but think that riddling a mind seemed easy compared to what his sister was doing.

Far away, Blythe bent to her task, inscribing once again the strange symbols in dissolvable ink made from a special type of gall that grew only on fir trees.

ψΦΦ∅⇊⇒⇑
≥≥∑Π⊒⊊χε
ΨΨ⊥βΓ≡≡
≡∍∍∍∑℘

"Good, yoss," Blythe whispered to herself.

There was a different key poem for each of the regions that the four bears visited. These were the middle lines of a love sonnet that Ezylryb had written for his beloved Lil.

Oh, the feverish eye, like a blazing star
Shines for you, my love
Calm my heart, be still my soul
Be still and Lil, 'tis you and only you

Jytte had given her grid code three, which she was applying to the lines of the poem. Blythe gasped in delight as the message came through loud and clear: *Coals soon ready at the ring. Send colliers.*

Nab MacNab sent as their escort his own son Conall. He was a friendly young wolf with the same gray pelt as his father. "I love going to the Ring. Wait till you see it."

"I don't understand," Stellan began, "how was it demolished by the earthquake but somehow came back?"

"Simple," Conall replied. "Another earthquake."

"Huh?" Froya said.

Conall laughed. "It was buried in the first earthquake, but when the second one happened, it was unburied. The ground fractured, and the volcanoes were roused and began erupting. They are back—all five of them, Dunmore, Morgan, H'rathghar, Kiel, and Stormfast."

"Stormfast, like the island?" Jytte asked, thinking of her father, Svern.

"Yes, I suppose so. Though I've never been there." A wistful look grazed Conall's green eyes. "Maybe if this war happens, I shall see it."

"You're wishing for war?" Third asked.

"Not really. But I would like to serve a great and noble cause. I mean, if the Ice Clock is not stopped, I shall see nothing of this world. And if that happens, we might be forced into the Distant Blue again."

"What was the Distant Blue like?" Froya asked.

"Oh, I don't know. I was only born after the MacNabs—I should say, the remnants of the MacNabs—returned. It took forever to sort out the old wolf clan territories. They had all been jumbled about. It was just after it was all sorted out that I was born." He paused and lifted his muzzle. "Do you smell it?"

There was an acrid scent in the air.

"I smell something," Jytte said.

"It's Dunmore erupting."

"You can tell?" Stellan asked.

"Oh yes, you learn these things once you become a guide to the ring. Each volcano has its own odor."

Led by Conall, they had begun to climb up to the high ridges, just as the clouds cleared and the stars began to sparkle beneath the Moon Claw. The Moon Claw was what the wolves called the first phase of a new moon. Like the owls, they had different names for the star constellations and the phases of the moon. The Golden Talons constellation of the owls was called by the wolves the Great Fangs. The Great Bear constellation was now called Lupus, the Great Wolf.

"There's the star ladder just rising." Conall raised one paw and pointed. "It goes to the Cave of Souls."

"And is that your Ursulana?" Third asked. "Our heaven and what the owls call glaumora. And yours is the Cave of Souls?"

"I believe so," Conall said. He chuckled softly and looked down at his feet. "Look at us—our feet, our paws, so different. Yet we stand here together on one earth. Yes, I sense that we might be on a very minor planet, circling a very ordinary star, the sun, but we can try to understand what makes each of our species special." Then he tipped his head back. "Under one sky and of one universe." Then he gasped in delight. "Just wait until you see the Ring. Soon!"

As they climbed, the stars in the midnight-blue sky started to fade and a dim rose-colored glow began to suffuse the sky in the north. "By the next ridge, you'll see the cones of the volcanoes and perhaps the flames of Dunmore."

And at the top of that next ridge, the four bears stopped suddenly, their eyes growing wide with wonder. Flames erupted from the ragged crowns of three volcanoes. Black rivers of lava poured down their sides.

"Makes your marrow shiver, doesn't it?" Conall asked.

All four bears were quiet for several moments.

The four bears did feel something in their bones that they had never before felt. It was as if perhaps, for this one moment, their species had merged—wolf and bear.

Stellan looked up. He saw a few owls scoring the sky.

"They couldn't have gotten here already, could they?"

"No. Just beginners. Half of them will get caught by a flame or a coal and perish. One has to be expert to fly these hot drafts of wind. Very tricky. Takes an expert collier to catch a coal on the fly or dive for coal in a lava slide. I'll show you something when we get to the Hot Gates."

"What are the Hot Gates?"

"The entrance to the ring. Where the Fengo will meet us."

The Fengo was awaiting. He was old and grizzled, a veteran of the trek to the Distant Blue and back, Conall had told them. He welcomed them to the ring. His voice was ragged, and his fur streaked with soot. But what drew the bears' attention was the spectacle on the towering bone mounds. Atop each one was a single wolf leaping high off the top of the mounds that they called *drumlyns* as they twisted and turned in the air. It was a dazzling spectacle.

"Ah," sighed the Fengo. "I see you are intrigued by these airborne wolves, who might even challenge the owls in their antics. There is a purpose to this seeming madness. With each leap, they monitor the plumes of ash and observe minute changes in the glow of the volcanoes' eruptions. This is valuable information, for it tells them when the coals are ripe, ready for harvesting, and they signal the colliers." He looked about and nodded to a gruesome figure that was on top of a smaller drumlyn. It was an owl cast in lava. "A stupid creature," the Fengo went on. "Caught in a molten flow." He then turned to Conall.

"And why have you brought these young bears here?"

Conall looked toward Stellan. "You see, sir, although the Nunquivik and the Ice Clock are far from the Beyond, all of us are in grave danger if the clock is not stopped. The clock is worshipped. And young'uns, or what they call Tick Tocks, very small cubs, are sacrificed to appease and honor it. A blood sacrifice to a false god. And the appetite for those young'uns could spread. All the creatures of these lands could be swept up for this

monstrous clock's hunger. You see, it feeds on fear, not faith."
Stellan spoke calmly, but Jytte was roiling inside. Their mother
was a prisoner in that Ice Clock. Coals, they knew, were important to owls as weapons. They fought with coals. Coals could
ignite flame swords that they carried into battle along with metal
cutlasses and ice weapons that were part of their arsenal and had
been from the time of the War of the Ice Talons. Coals were the
fuel for their forging fires.

"So the true colliers will come back and perhaps teach
these young'uns how it's really done." He tipped his head toward
the owls flying over the volcanoes. "They haven't visited much
since our return." He sighed wistfully. "I suppose Soren and
Otulissa are too old now to dive the coals."

"A bit, sir," Stellan replied.

"And," Jytte added, "Otulissa lost one eye in the battle with
the blue owls from the Middle Kingdom."

"Oh yes, those were hard times. That was not long before our
evacuation to the Distant Blue. And now we are on the brink of
a new war."

Stellan felt glad that at least the Fengo had used the word
we unlike Chieftain Duncan MacDuncan, who did not seem to
feel that the threat of the Ice Clock was any of his clan's
concern.

The bears were soon directed to a den for the night, but in
truth, they were so mesmerized by the dazzling sight of the flames
and the rivers of lava that they could not sleep. They had come
from a place of ice and now they were in one of fire. Spectacular

fire, where flames and wolves gyrated in a wild dance against the night.

It was almost dawn when they finally fell to sleep. Flames painted their dreams with fountains of hot glowing coals and cascades of sparks sizzling in the night—all except for Third, whose dreams took him far from the Ring of Sacred Volcanoes.

The terrain was unlike any Third had ever set a paw on since being in the Beyond. The ground was soft. He was in that marshy region, the Slough that Alasdair had described when they were listening to the skreeleen. The words that Alasdair had uttered when they were listening to the skeeleen now echoed in his dream. *The Sark of the Slough. She toyed with fire, disturbed the order . . . disturbed the order . . . disturbed the order . . . disturbed the order.* It was as if Third had entered an echo chamber of his own dream. But this was no "chamber." *I am in the Slough,* Third thought. *I am in the cavern of the Sark of the Slough.* He wound his way through the tangle of connecting dens in the cavern. There seemed to be dens within dens that led to other dens. Skin bags stuffed with herbs hung on antlers jammed into cracks in the walls. And everywhere there were clay pots and vessels. He finally came to one in which the ragged figure of an ancient she-wolf bent over a jug. Instinctively, Third knew that this jug did not contain herbs or any material, really. Not like the skin bags when he had walked into the first den of the cavern. The wolf was sniffing. Sniffing a dream? No, this was something different— something real. A memory! *This is a memory jug!* The she-wolf looked up. She had a strange skittish eye that seemed to look everywhere but nowhere at once. But she fixed Third with her single good eye. *Yes, this is real,* she seemed to say to Third. *But I am not.*

A ghost?

Call me what you will—gillygaskin, scroom . . . I've mounted the star ladder, but it is too soon for . . . too soon.

She whispered into the jug. Her voice seemed to break.

Third sat straight up. "What is it?" Stellan asked. "You look as if you've seen a gilly."

"I have and I don't want to see another! Alasdair!"

By this time, Jytte and Froya were awake.

"A dream about Alasdair?" Froya asked.

"We have to save her," Third said. His voice seethed with fear. "There is a slink melf . . ." His throat seemed to lock on the words.

CHAPTER 24

Cell Block Six

Lago and her sister, Illya, had just entered the den with the words *Bear Containment Facility* printed above the doorframe. Illya turned to Lago.

"Follow me to cell block six." She then swiped her long, luxuriant tail across her muzzle as a signal for complete silence.

The only illumination when they entered cell block six was that of a sliver of a new moon that passed through the bars. There was a pile of what appeared to be tattered old pelts in one corner. But gradually, Lago realized it was a bear with its back turned toward them. This must be Uluk Uluk. He was unaware of their presence. Hunched over, he was muttering to himself. "Him and his cursed overcoil . . . never a good idea. Never was! Never will be . . . always throws off the action between the crown and the ratchet wheel. Brequet, will you ever learn? Yes . . . yes. I know you made the queen watch. And look what happened to her. Lost her head, she did. Too bad . . . Of course you'll never learn. You've been dead for thousands of years."

Tears came to Illya's eyes. He was lost in the mists of clock history. He was indeed a shadow of his former self—a raggedy shadow at that. He must have lost his sense of smell, for surely he would have picked up their scent by now. She dragged the sharp claws of one paw against the stone floor. Lago looked at her in alarm, for the sound was distinct, yet Uluk Uluk did not betray the barest hint that he was alert to their presence. *He must be almost deaf as well*, Illya thought.

She now coughed loudly. He turned around slowly.

"You!" That was all he said, and the monocle fell from his eye. It was as if he didn't even see Illya. He held a tiny spring in one paw and a small notched disc in the other.

"Still fiddling with the Brequet, I see." She sighed. "Nothing changes." The old bear did not wear his years well. He was bent with age. His paws trembled, but Great Ursus she still loved him. *What a foolish thing I am!*

Uluk Uluk turned his head slowly around. Blinked, then roared.

"EXCEPT YOU! You seem to have a gift for that. For changing." He stood up, glaring at Illya. He was so thin and frail that his stained and tattered pelt seemed four times too large for him. It draped in ripples over his gaunt frame. "Why are you here, and who's this?"

"My sister, Lago," Illya replied calmly.

"Eh?" He cupped his paw to his ear.

"Lago, my sister!" she said louder.

"Oh, now she's fallen in love with me too."

"Hardly!" snapped Lago.

"Why are you here?"

"I went to the Ice Clock."

"You what?"

"I went to the Ice Clock." Her voice almost broke as she said this. *Has he nothing but contempt for me?* thought Illya.

"How'd you do that?" Uluk Uluk asked scornfully.

Illya took a deep breath. "I went as my other self, my Ki-hi-ru self, a bear. I now realize that is no self at all, but I went as Galilya. I took all that I had learned from you about clock-making and timepieces and I became Galilya, the Mystress of the Chimes."

"You? The Mystress of the Chimes!"

"Inga died. She was stupid."

"She was stupid, so you say? And you, I suppose, were smarter," he said scathingly.

She was determined to not let him provoke her and replied evenly, "Indeed. I figured out the bungvik."

His monocle, which he had just replaced moments before to get a better look at the two foxes, dropped from his eye. "You figured out the bungvik?"

"Not only that, I figured out how they are planning to funnel it through the baffles."

Uluk Uluk lifted his muzzle into the air. He could be such an arrogant bear. "Now, how would you know this, Galilya?" It annoyed Lago that he called her sister by this name. She wanted to yell, *Call her Illya!* But she dared not.

"I swam through it."

"You swam the baffles!"

"I did, and here is their plan."

Uluk Uluk blinked and once more his monocle fell out.

"Get me some sealscap parchment. I'll show you."

"Yes, yes, of course." The change in Uluk Uluk was remarkable. Although his shape hadn't shifted, when he returned with a sheet of sealscap and a charred stick for drawing, it was as if he was a new bear, if not a new creature that had emerged.

"Show me!" he said eagerly as he spread out the sealscap on a table.

Illya climbed up on the table. She gripped the charred stick and began to quickly sketch a latticework of lines. "You see, this is the central matrix of the baffling system."

"Yes, yes, the matrix!" Uluk Uluk boomed.

"We always assumed that when the bungvik broke, it would flood everything below the Ice Cap of the Ublunkyn—everything to the south. But not so."

"How not?"

"Have you ever heard of *mydlsvarls?*"

"The old legends of the mydlsvarl serpents from the time of Svree?"

Illya nodded.

"Yes, of course, they are like tunnels, gongs, they called them in Old Krakish. Not quite frost and not quite mist."

"There is a natural network of these mydlsvarls in the outer part of the Nunquivik Sea. They connect conveniently with the N'yrthghar Straits. The pouches of the serpents are called bungs. The Grand Patek plans to direct the bungvik waters through the baffling system to the—"

"To the N'yrthghar Straits," Uluk Uluk finished her sentence.

"Exactly. But he has to wait until the conditions are perfect—the tides, the state of the ice, the winds, the phase of the moon. The clock can reveal this perfect time. That is what all the calculations are for—not to predict the next Great Melting but to determine when the most favorable moment is for releasing the waters of the bungvik."

"So how do we stop this?" Uluk Uluk asked.

Illya raised a brow slightly. "*We*," she thought. *He said "we"!* "Two possibilities. Somehow we get someone to redirect the baffles. But too many blue seals have already been killed just making sure the baffles work as the Grand Patek wants them to work." She thought of Jameson. "Or we get the key."

"The key to the clock? But it's in the Den of Forever Frost."

Illya nodded. "But there have been rumors that it no longer is."

"What kind of rumors?"

"Rumors that a rebel bear called Svern—"

"SVERN!" Uluk Uluk exclaimed. "Svern is active again?"

Illya nodded.

"If any bear could get the key, it would be Svern." And then Uluk Uluk's eyes grew misty. He recalled two young bears. Cubs they were when he first met them. There was a scent that seemed familiar to him. Now what were their names? Jytte and Stellan—that was it! Extraordinarily bright. He had sent them to the clock. Most likely dead by now, he thought wistfully. But he had sent them for a good cause. Why did he think of them now when he thought of Svern? Could they have been his cubs?

CHAPTER 25

A Figure in the Mists

Svern raced as fast as he could to the site where Svenna awaited him. Admittedly, he had thrown caution to the wind. Svenna did not have the coding skills to inform or expand on how she had come to be there. He just knew she was there. She was there, and Blue Bear was not. He didn't understand why he was not there. But right now he had only one focus in mind. Svenna! He couldn't wait to tell her that their cubs lived! Not only lived but had achieved the impossible—penetrated the Den of Forever Frost and retrieved the key!

A thick mist had swept in from the north. He tipped his head up to the sky. It was as if a veil had dropped over the Great Bear constellation. He wanted to identify her star, the heel star for which she was named, as he was named for the knee star. *Heel follows knee*, she would always say. But now he was following her. He tipped his head up again. How he had looked forward to pointing out the skipping stars, Jytte and Stellan, from which their cubs had taken names. But he moved on. There was no time to waste. He couldn't travel fast enough to get to her. His beloved Svenna, whom he had never loved enough, treasured enough. All that he wanted was for Svenna, the cubs, and himself to be together again in this world. But would this world last? The key was safe in the tree, but soon they must consider going to war.

The details he received from Blythe so far were scant. She had to be very cautious in her coded transmissions. It wouldn't do to have any of these messages picked up by a slipgizzle. And there were slipgizzzles throughout the Hoolian kingdoms. Of this he was sure. There was a suspect he had heard about from other Yinquis in the Beyond. The Beyond was what Yinquis called "porous." The clans newly returned from the Distant Blue could be easy to infiltrate. One would have thought their rigid order and protocols might be difficult for an enemy operative. But wolves were also known to carry old grudges for decades. The best slipgizzles were creatures with grudges. However, there was also another aspect to wolf culture that could account for a wolf turning spy. Wolves were obsessed with hierarchies and order, and there was a lust with some wolves to belong to the most inner circle within the clan chieftain's pack. They wanted desperately to believe that they were just a wolf's whisker away from an exclusive group that held the real power. And for that they would sell their wolf souls. With this passion for power, an animal could be lured into doing very evil things.

But now, just now, he saw a figure in the mists. *Svenna!*

The mists suddenly cleared. The stars shone. Svern lifted his arms high. With one paw, he pointed at two stars skipping behind the heel star. "Jytte, Stellan!" he cried out. "Our cubs!"

Svenna roared with happiness. "Dearest Svern." She began rushing toward him.

But suddenly he was gone. He simply vanished. It was as if the ice had swallowed him. Svenna looked about stunned. How could this have happened? She began to beat the ice furiously. Pounding on it with all her might, crying out, "Svern, Svern." She raged, her voice became hoarse, and the name of her beloved turned ragged in the night.

"Let her pound," a bear said with a soft snarl.

"You don't want me to go up and get her, Captain?" another bear said. He had a stripe of blood proudly displayed across his chest. He was holding an ice club with which he had knocked Svern unconscious. "I mean, I thought she'd come through that trap with him."

"No." The other bear inhaled sharply. "Well, I'll be swoggled." He looked up at the bear with the club. "Byornyk, we got ourselves a real VIB here."

"A what?"

"VIB—very important bear!"

"Really?"

"Yes, look at the top of his head. See that bubbly black skin."

"Yeah, looks burned."

"You bet, Byornyk. They were burned off in a black ice ort before he escaped. We got ourself a Yinqui. Not just any Yinqui, I would say." He paused a moment. "And you know what else?"

"What, Captain?"

"He killed my brother—Dark Fang." He chuckled. "Oh, we're going to have fun with this one."

"He's not dead, is he?"

"Oh, no, what fun would that be if he were dead? You gave him a good blow. He'll come to in time."

What the two bears didn't realize was that Svern had already come to. His first thought of course was one of relief. Relief that they had not caught Svenna. His next thought was that these two bears, though not the brightest—especially Byornyk—had booby-trapped him. He wondered if they had booby-trapped Blue Bear as well. *Ursuskadamus*, he prayed they would not get Svenna. He had to banish any thoughts of her right now. He had to get out of here. But what was *here*? That was the question.

Beyond the scent of these two bears—Captain and Byornyk—there was nothing. But he actually could feel some dewy drops of moisture forming on his nose. Odd in such a dry place. He had to think about this for a while. The two Roguer bears were busy eating a piece of dried seal liver. Svern opened one eye just a slit. It was all he could do to keep from gasping. This was a mydlsvarl—a gong. He had no idea there were such tunnels beneath the ice in in these parts of the Hrath'ghar. This did not augur well. It suddenly dawned on him what this could mean. It was not simply a Great Melting that the Ice Clock could predict. That was all nonsense. What it was would be a great flooding engineered by the bears of the Ice Clock. A devastation created specifically to destroy the world beyond the Nunquivik to the south—the world of Ga'Hoole. In the time of the legends, it was said that there was a coiled serpent called Mydl that held vast amounts of water in pouches—or bungviks. When the earth quaked, the Mydl writhed and uncoiled. The pent-up waters would spill from its pouches. There must be an enormous pouch beneath site of the Ice Clock. A true bungvik! And in the right season—say, between the last of the seal moon and the first of the Ice Cracking Moons—it gave the bears of the Ice Clock a very direct route for these pent-up waters of the bungvik—unless, of course, the clock was stopped!

Of one thing he was certain. These "gongs" or mydlsvarls were not structures made by bears. These had happened most likely after the Great Melting and in the present time. It could have been the earthquake that wreaked havoc in this region some years before that had opened them here or cleared the way for them to form. The bears of the Ice Clock had realized this. They had been handed a gift, so to speak, by the earthquakes. And the Hrathlands, as some called them, were periodically tormented by quakes. The land was often left jumbled, discombobulated—mountains flattened. New ones rising, glaciers shattered. Perhaps this was how these frost tunnels had come to this region. How long had they been here? When had the bears of the Ice Clock discovered them?

CHAPTER 26

Fracture

Born in the Distant Blue, Alasdair since a very young age had a longing, a yearning, for a place in the Beyond that she never knew. It was as if she could smell this place without ever having been there. It was like a scent thread that streamed through her. When the MacDuncan clan had returned and she was still just a pup, she had been made a scout because of her extremely sharp sense of smell. She seemed to be able to track down the trail of any creature. Not only that, she could pick up the scent of a season before it actually arrived. She could smell the Moon of the Salmon before the salmon began to swim up the streams in the fall. She could catch a whiff of the mossflowers in the spring before they had pushed up from the ground during the Mossflower Moon. But there was one tantalizing smell that had nothing to do with any season. It was an earthy smell—of clay, of mud long hardened from streams. It had taken her several years to finally find the source. It was in the Slough, and the closer she got to it the more fearful she became, for this Slough was known for only one thing—the witch known as the Sark of the Slough. Even when the wolves were hunting, a *byrgiss* formation would give it a wide berth. But finally Alasdair knew she could not avoid it any longer, and some moons before, she had gone there, to its very center, and discovered the ruins of the Sark of the Slough's cavern. The Sark's old kiln, where she had fired her pots, her jugs and pitchers, was in shambles. Yet Alasdair recognized it immediately. She had heard the stories about the crazy old witch wolf who made all manner of vessels and whispered her secrets and magical charms into them. But she was also known as a healer.

The clan wolves were profoundly superstitious, particularly of knowledge that was not related to hunting or territory. They believed that the Sark had "disturbed the order," the order of the Great Chain by which the clans organized every aspect of their lives. When Alasdair finally got up her nerve to enter the cave, she instantly felt wrapped in the *hwlyn*, the spirit of the Sark. She had found her pack! Although it was only a pack of one.

Whenever Alasdair could, she traveled to the cave. She had to be careful, however. If the wolves knew, they would become leery of her. In the wreckage of the cave, she began to find shards of more pots and bowls and jugs. She started to piece them together, to make them whole again. She had an amazing instinct for mending them. She created beautiful shapes, the ones the

Sark must have originally envisioned. And when she had completed putting together the first jug, she knew instantly that there were no charms, no dark magic in them, but only memories and stories. Memories of the amazing wolf Faolan. A slightly deformed foot had deemed him a malcadh and cast him out of the pack he was born into. Left him to die on a *tummfraw*. But he had survived. Survived and been selected to be Watch wolf at the Ring of Sacred Volcanoes. When the time of the great earthquakes came, he had led the clans out of the Beyond to the Distant Blue. By the time the clans had returned, he had been long dead. But part of his story was in the first jug.

It was only in the previous moon, the Frost Star Moon, that Alasdair discovered a story relating to herself. She caught her breath as she put into place the last fragment of the broken jug. She knew instantly that this was a pot about her, even though she and the Sark had never shared life on this earth together. But the story was here, in the burnished glaze of the jug. It was as if an ancient voice swirled up from its shadowy depths and in a dim whisper said, *I was born a malcadh. My defect was ugliness and my skittering eye, and yet, although my mother's form was perfect, my mother was a malcadh as well for she was twisted inside her head. On the inside, she was as ugly as I am on the outside. I always thought it was a blessing that I was as ugly as my mother was beautiful, for then no wolf would try to make me his mate. But now here is my deepest secret. A male, a good male yet one who decided to be an outclanner and never joined a pack, fell in love with me.*

He died soon after I gave birth. I knew I could not take care of her alone. I knew it would be a hardship for her to endure with the teasing of having me as a mother. I am not a particularly good hunter. I can hardly get enough for myself. So I left her with the MacDonegal clan. She grew up. She found a mate in the MacDuncan clan and went off I think to the Distant Blue. It was the hardest thing I ever had to do. But it was the right choice, I believe.

"The Sark was my grandmother!" Alasdair whispered to herself.

It had been almost two moons since Alasdair had made this remarkable discovery. She had not had time to come back. During the hunger moon, she rarely got a break but was always out scouting for any herd or single animal she could find. However, finally, she was able to get back to the Slough. When she arrived, she picked up a new scent. Not prey, at least not any kind that would interest a wolf. It was an odd smell. Slightly bearish but not exactly. Not like the four bears she had met and guided to the chieftain. Those she would have recognized. And was there a whiff of MacHeath? That was an alarming thought. She thought about the four bears now. She had heard they were at the Ring of Sacred Volcanoes. This actually had irritated Duncan MacDuncan a great deal. He had been stomping around day and night complaining about the ridiculous MacNab clan and how they squandered their resources and next thing you knew they would be wanting to hunt with our byrgisses. *Damn fools*, he had thundered. *And now promising fighting coals from the Sacred Ring. I tell you nothing's sacred anymore! We're giving away too much! We need to stay out of bear business and all that nonsense about some Ice Clock!*

There of course was nothing to be done about this. So Alasdair decided to go back to the place she felt now was home—the caverns of the Sark of the Slough.

Sometimes she wondered if perhaps like the Sark's mate, her own grandfather, she was really more of an outclanner wolf than a clan one. But to leave a clan was a momentous decision. She was certain that the chieftain would take it as an insult, a personal affront. He was not at all like his own great-grandfather who had been the chieftain and died long before the wolves had gone to the Distant Blue. He craved attention. He wanted to be revered. Alasdair secretly felt that he was not. And it rankled Duncan MacDuncan greatly.

Now, as she carefully pawed over the fragments of another jug, Alasdair caught a freakish scent. *Freakish* was the only word she could think of. It seemed to be at odds with everything in this cavern, which had to do with beauty and memory and the incredible loveliness of her grandmother the Sark of the Slough. A shadow of a single wolf slid across the opening of the cave. Then another shadow. One that was distinctly recognizable. A crescent was bitten from one of the wolf's ears. *Quint!* The leader of the MacHeath slink melf!

A slink melf was entering the cavern. Her grandmother's cavern. Alasdair couched farther into the cave. She was behind a small mound of shards waiting for her care, her attention—waiting for the pots to be mended, the memories to be completed, the stories to be told.

"The wolf king will be proud!" Quint snarled, and leaped.

CHAPTER 27

Weeping at the Star Ladder

Rags flipped her head around and upside down to look back as she flew over the four racing bears. Almost keeping up with her, they were just blurs in the light snow that swirled over the land. From her vantage point, she could see the humps of hillocks that, according to Third, marked the place on the map where the Sark's cavern was. She plunged down and angled her wings. Third looked up.

"Two points south and east?" he bayed.

"Confirmed," Rags hooted. "Sark's cavern less than a quarter league to port."

Rags and the four bears had left the Ring of Sacred Volcanoes at dawn. The urgency of Third's dream as he had described it propelled them at a speed that the wolves would have called press paw. But they were all filled with a mounting dread that something horrific had happened to their trusted guide Alasdair. Nevertheless they felt torn. Especially Stellan. They had accomplished much: the Frost Beaks unit from Silverveil as well as the services of their blacksmith Gwynn. And from the MacNabs, they had gained entry to the Sacred Volcanoes, where the Fengo himself promised to allow access to the collier owls. But this detour to Alasdair would delay them, and the Ice Clock was still ticking. It had to be stopped. There were no hours or even seconds to be wasted. And yet he remembered so well that peculiar grief, the desolation he sensed in Alasdair and now suddenly that fear he had felt for her. They must go. There was no choice.

The marshy terrain of the Slough slowed their pace but not their determination. Third was in the lead. It was as if in his dream a map had been etched in his brain. "We follow the river due south. When we get to a place where once there were trees, then we head east."

"Once there were trees?" Jytte asked. "The trees are gone? Why? How are we to see them if they're are gone?"

"They were swept away in the big earthquake," Third replied.

It was not long until they saw the once-there-were-trees place. Random stumps poked up from the ground. Stellan approached one and crouched down. "Look! There's green poking out of this stump . . . It's as if a little tree is coming back, growing out of the ruins of the dead tree."

"A gilly tree?" Froya asked.

"No, a real little tree," Stellan replied.

"There's one here too," Jytte called out where she stood over another stump.

"A miracle!" Froya exclaimed.

"Yes," Third said. "But we must hurry. We must." He could only hope that they would find another miracle waiting for them. He dashed off due east. The other bears followed.

It was twilight when they arrived at the Sark's cave. The stars were just breaking out.

"So this is it?" Stellan said as he stood by the wreckage of the Sark's kiln. Then they heard a terrible moaning from inside the cave where Third had already dashed.

The three other bears stopped short at the wrenching sight before them. Third sat on the blood-soaked floor of the cave with Alasdair's head in his lap.

"She's dying," Third whispered as tears ran down his face. "I found her right here. She dragged herself here from deep inside."

"I . . . I want to see the Cave of Souls . . . see . . . my . . . my grand . . . she is waiting, but first . . . before I go . . ."

"Try not to talk, Alasdair."

"No, I have things to tell, but . . . See, the Great Wolf points to the Cave of Souls. There's the spirit trail to the star ladder and . . . and Skaarsgard, the guide." She began to cough. Foamy blood dribbled from her mouth.

"Hush," Third said softly, and stroked her head. But a fierce glare suddenly sparkled in Alasdair's blue eyes. "Quint . . . Quint."

"Quint?" Third asked.

"Go . . . go to the Namara . . . the Namara!" Her eyes rolled back into her head. There was one last breath. A faint breeze stirred in the cave, and with it a spirit passed. Alasdair, granddaughter of the Sark of the Slough, was gone.

The four bears were quiet for a long time. They then had a sense of what needed to be done. It was almost as if Stellan had riddled her dying thoughts.

"We must take her body deeper into the cave. We don't want scavengers to get to her."

So with Stellan carrying the body of Alasdair gently as if she were just a cub, they went deeper into the cave. At first, they felt that perhaps there were other bones in this cave. But the deeper they went, it was not bones that they found but shards of broken pottery. Gradually, they began to pick out in the dim light perhaps a dozen or more pots that seemed to have been reassembled from those shards.

"This is where we must put her," Stellan said. "Here with these pots." Tenderly, he lay her down on top of a mass of shards that were not merely discarded but seemed to be awaiting mending. They sat in complete silence for another moment and then began to make their way toward the opening of the cave.

When they stepped into the deep blue of the night, Jytte exclaimed, "There it is!" She was pointing toward a constellation just above the Great Wolf that was rising high in the eastern sky. "The star ladder to the Cave of Souls!"

"And look. There is a blue mist gathered at the bottom of the ladder!" Third exclaimed. "A mist exactly the color of Alasdair's eyes!"

"At the top! See the top of the ladder!" Stellan cried out. A starry wolf appeared to be waiting for Alasdair.

And no one needed to say it, but they all felt it. This was the Sark of the Slough awaiting her granddaughter from the Beyond, to lead her to yet another Beyond.

Stellan felt a great peace surge through him. The howling of the skreeleen, of Greer da Greer and her story of the Sark came back to him. How vividly he remembered those tears trembling in Alasdair's eyes. *The story is complete*, he thought. *Finally complete.*

Stellan rose up. "To the Namara!"

The Namara

CHAPTER 28

A Secret Language

No sooner had the four bears left the Slough, the cave of the Sark, and the earthly remains of the lovely Alasdair, than an immense blizzard began to blow. This did not stop them in the least. They were, after all, bears of the Nunquivik, accustomed to the strongest winds known and the fiercest blizzards. Drifts that would swallow wolves or blinding winds with barreling snow that erased the horizons of any landscape did not intimidate these bears. Stellan had taken the lead now. This would be the third clan they had visited, and when this clan heard that Alasdair had been murdered, he sensed that this might turn the tide for them.

Quint . . . ? Was it a word, or was it a name? Did it matter? But in fact, word or name, they must take it to the Namara. And Stellan sensed it might be crucial to their task of forming this alliance. *Quint* . . . the word rattled in Stellan's mind. Quint—whatever it was could be a key, another key, Stellan realized, as important as the one tucked away in the Great Tree. A key to a deadly secret, perhaps, in this enigmatic land.

They were trying to make as good time as they could as they headed toward the MacNamara territory in the northern reaches of the Beyond that was near a point jutting out into the Sea of Hoolemere. But finally after a night, then a day and another morning, they were exhausted and had to stop. Rags herself was too tired and had spent the last several hours perched on first Stellan's back, then Jytte's, and now Froya's. She tried to grip hard with her talons to their fur. Her talons were sharp, and she worried about puncturing their skin. But soon she mastered the "fur grip," as she thought of it.

They found a den and nearby a musk ox. His leg was badly broken, and he was in a great deal of pain. "I think we should end his pain," Jytte said. They were all very hungry. She looked at the others, and they nodded.

"Wait just a second," Froya said.

"What?" Jytte replied. "Wait? I'm starving."

"*Lochinvyrr?*" Stellan asked.

"Yes," Froya nodded.

As part of their studies of the Beyond. they had read about the wolf ritual of lochinvyrr. It was a ceremony practiced by the wolves when an animal they had attacked was dying. It had been described to them by Otulissa as an instinct as much as a ritual. An urge that flowed through them to acknowledge the dying animal's value. It became a demonstration of respect for the dying animal.

"How do you do it?" Third asked.

"I'm not exactly sure. I think we all have to get down on our knees. Then, one by one, we look into the creature's eyes," Froya tried to explain as best she could.

And so they did, each one of them, and when the last bear, Jytte, rose up, Stellan sliced quickly with his claw, opening the life-giving artery in the musk ox's neck. It died instantly.

They ate until they were full, then dug out a snow den near the creature's body. Third turned to his sister, Froya. "Froya, you've studied the history of the MacNamaras the most. Tell us what must we know, for Alasdair said we should go to the Namara. It was a slink melf that killed her—a MacHeath slink melf."

Froya took a deep breath. "You see, it is because of the MacHeaths that the MacNamara clan began. The MacHeaths were and still are *tragten wolfyn*, that means—"

"Terror wolves!" Jytte murmured.

"Yes, they especially terrorized the females in the clan, who were virtual slaves. The first of the MacNamara clan was a wolf called Hordweard. She killed her mate Dunleavy MacHeath. But this was all more than one thousand years ago, in the time of Hoole, the first owl king of the Great Tree."

When there is a blizzard as strong as the one sweeping across the Beyond, there is no day or night. So for many hours, Froya told them about the MacNamara clan. How the word *Namara* had actually been the name of a she-wolf, her own mother, who had been slain by Dunleavy MacHeath. That the word itself had come to mean over the centuries maker of strong spirits. It was a clan in which females held all the most high-ranking positions. They were known for their hunting skills, but also like the owls of Ga'Hoole they performed noble deeds. "They spoke no words but true ones," Froya murmured, and began to repeat the oath of honor of the owls. The three other bears joined her softly. "Their purpose was to right all wrongs, to make strong the weak, mend the broken, vanquish the proud, and make powerless those who abused the frail."

Froya paused. "The MacNamara clan are all strong fighters. Alasdair told us about the MacHeath slink melf. They need to know. Soon!" She paused for several seconds. "And there is one more thing."

"What's that?" Stellan asked.

"They have a secret language all of their own. It is a language that only the females speak. It is called *Banuil Caint*, which means she-wolf talk."

"Do you know any words, Froya?"

"Not a word," she said. "No one does except the she-wolves of the MacNamara clan. It seems that it's impossible for a male wolf to even learn or pronounce these words. It's as if their brain is not made for it."

The weather eventually cleared. The bears and Rags were well rested, and the wind had changed. There was now a bit of a tail wind. "This is easy!" Rags exclaimed. "I'm not going to tire myself out flying back to keep up with your slow pace." She churred.

They had all become deeply fond of Rags. She was such a smart little owl, and to think that her mother had left her. Froya and Third especially felt a deep sympathy for her, as they had had the worst mum in the world—Taaka. They had shared their own experiences with Rags and the little spotted owl had sighed and wilfed slightly. "I thought I was the only one. I guess you can say we belong to the Bad Mum Club!"

Stellan had said nothing at the time, but he felt it was a bit sad for such a young owl to be so cynical. This perhaps had been Rags's strength. Helped her "soldier through." *Soldiering through*, it was a term Stellan and Jytte's mum, Svenna, often said. *Mum . . . will we ever see her again?* Stellan wondered, and felt his eyes fill with tears.

CHAPTER 29

Svenna Carries On

"Why does a puffin cross the straits?" The cackling cry came out of the thick fog of the Ice Narrows.

"Because . . . because . . . a chicken already had?"

"Oh, little Dumpy, you are brilliant."

"What's a chicken, Mum?"

"How should I know? I'm just a dumb cluck." Then there was a deafening chorus of clucking puffins.

Svenna ignored the puffins as she swam through the Ice Narrows that had not yet frozen. She was exhausted, but she would not let up despite the adverse current slowing her pace. Svern had vanished as if by magic—and Great Ursus, she prayed it wasn't some kind of ancient sorcery of hagsfiends. Could they be back? Svenna knew there was only one thing to do. Go to the Great Ga'Hoole Tree. Svern had known the owls, had fought in the last battle of the owls against the Pure Ones at the Battle of

Fire and Ice, as it was often called. The bears of the Northern Kingdoms and the owls of the Northern Kingdoms had fought valiantly together. The time had come again. Something strange and evil had felled her dear Svern.

The ridiculous cackling of the puffins grew dimmer. Then at last she was out of the Ice Narrows. She spied solid ice ahead. It was just a quarter of a league to the ice shelf of the Sea of Hoolemere.

When she climbed onto the ice, she knew she was almost there. Her heart was pounding as she flopped down for just a few brief minutes—minutes, seconds, hours, milliseconds—that part of her life was over. She was no longer a slave of the clock . . . but what if the Ice Clock enslaved the whole world? Or destroyed it? The bungvik . . . Could Svern's disappearance be connected in some way to the bungvik?

At the same time, Svenna was wrestling with the horror of total annihilation, her former enslaver, Galilya, now Illya, was explaining just this to Uluk Uluk. "It would be extinction, Uluk. Complete and utter extinction—except for them!"

Svenna herself, as she contemplated this eradication of all creatures, began to sob on the ice, sob so violently that she didn't hear the scratch of talons as a tiny owl landed.

"Bear, why are you crying?" Sobs were so racking Svenna's body that the little pygmy had to shout finally, "Why, why are you crying, beautiful bear?"

Finally, Svenna looked up. She blinked. Another tear spilled from her dark eyes and froze instantly. "Who are you?"

"Rosie, pygmy, a rather noisy flyer in comparison to other owl species. But your crying drowned out my wing beats, I daresay."

"Are you from the Great Tree?"

"Yes, yes! I can be your guide. That's one of my jobs. I fly surveillance over this part of the Sea of Hoolemere. You see I'm a HALO flyer."

"What?"

"HALO—high altitude, low opening. Those are the conditions that we are used for. When it's thick of fog or heavy cloud cover, I can drop down quickly. No one sees me approaching or, in your case, hears me."

"Well, you have to guide me to the Great Tree. This is urgent!"

"Follow me. I'll fly low."

Rosie began skimming just inches above the ice as the thick fog roiled around them.

The fog began to thin a bit as they approached the island of Hoole. The tree was just becoming visible.

"There it is!" Rosie began to make a soft little *too-too-too* sound. Svenna looked up in awe. She had never in her life seen such a tree. It was not simply enormous, but its limbs spread out across the sky, across the earth, or so it seemed. From the limbs hung vines of white berries that swayed in a gentle wind. It appeared as if the tree was almost breathing. Svenna stopped. The sight was mesmerizing.

"Come along! Come along! Parliament is in emergency session."

As Svenna entered the parliament hollow, her first thought was how many different kinds of owls there were—at least twenty different species of all sizes and colors. Then she spotted one of the smaller owls, a white-faced owl with a fringe of tawny feathers. And she immediately knew. *So this is Soren!* Svenna thought. Soren, the fabled leader of the Great Ga'Hoole Tree, seemed rather small and quite elderly. But size had nothing to do with it in this world of owls. Some said that the barn owl was the greatest leader since the first king, Hoole, son of Siv and Hrath. But Svenna was still somewhat astonished when she saw him, perched not on a throne of any kind but a curved birch branch. He wore no crown or jewels as the Grand Patek did. He was merely an owl, a very old owl. His plumage slightly faded, his talons gnarled with age. He peered at her with dim eyes, not glossy like the other younger barn owls in the parliament.

"Come closer, my dear. I hear you have some startling news. It seems to be a night for that."

Svenna was unsure of what else he was referring to. "My name is Svenna. I am from the Sven clan in the—"

Before she could finish the sentence, there was a reverberation that passed through the hollow. "Aaaah . . . awwwh . . ." The entire parliament exclaimed softly.

"The clan of Svenka!"

"Yes." She nodded modestly. "And the mate of Svern."

"Svern?" A much younger barn owl gasped. This owl bore a close resemblance to Soren, and Svenna felt she must be his daughter.

"Yes, Svern."

"And how is Svern?" the young barn owl asked.

"Not well, I fear. That is why I'm here." The young owl staggered on her perch. "I think he has been captured."

"Captured!" the owl shrieked.

"Steady, dear. Steady, Blythe."

"Oh, Da, I was wondering why I hadn't received any messages for the last few nights. Nothing . . . nothing at all."

Soren leaned forward from his perch. "Tell us what you know, Svenna."

And so she told him the story. By the time she finished, it was as if the very air of the parliament roiled with a fear so toxic the owls were almost afraid to breathe. It was paralyzing.

Soren finally broke the silence. "The bears of the Nunquivik must be on the move. They want to stop us and they want the key."

All eyes were turned to Soren and Otulissa, who perched near him. They all had one thought. Those two owls, the barn owl and the spotted owl, were the only ones in the entire tree who knew where the key was hidden.

Soren swung around. "Blythe, any messages from the young bears Stellan, Jytte . . ." Svenna felt something seize within her. It was as if her heart had stopped and her breath had locked.

"Stellan and Jytte!" Svenna gasped. The entire parliament shook. "You know my cubs?"

"Yes, Svenna. They came here," Otulissa replied with as much calm she could muster.

"I . . . I . . . don't understand. They are alive? They live?"

"They live very well, madam. They are brave, courageous young bears. They along with two other yosses rescued the key from the Den of Forever Frost. They and their companions, Third and Froya, are now on a mission gathering allies for our cause, or I should say for war, I fear . . ."

But by this time, Svenna was swaying on her feet. "I must sit down, sir. You see I was never really sure if they were still alive . . ." Her voice dwindled away.

"Please, madam, of course. This must be a shock. A pleasant one. But these four young bears are quite remarkable."

"Yes," Svenna said in a vague voice. But would they even know her? Would she know them? And where had the other two bears come from?

CHAPTER 30

Two Old Warriors

In the dim light of a new dawn, as the rest of the tree's inhabitants settled into their hollows, Soren and Otulissa met in the innermost part of the late Ezylryb's hollow. It was a place where these two old owls often retreated to think and discuss critical matters of the tree. Ezylryb's ancient battle claws hung on a hook forged by Bubo, the great blacksmith of the tree, now long dead. There was a soft, somewhat moth-ravaged velvet pillow that Octavia, the long-deceased nest-maid snake of Ezylryb, would often coil up on for a rest. There were some of the volumes he had written—his poetry, his memoirs of the War of the Ice Talons, which he had fought in nearly a century ago. It was a place where memory was stirred, thinking was clarified, and hopes emboldened. But it was not a place for useless nostalgia, as Otulissa often reminded her old friend, should he veer into that when he spoke of his mentor, Ezylryb.

"So here we are, Otulissa. Two old warriors ourselves now. How old do you think Ezylryb was when he fought?"

Otulissa cut him off. "Doesn't matter, Soren. What matters is that we are on the brink of war. The reports coming in from the warblers and the other HALO flyers are not good. There is a steady flow of Roguer bears and we now know of at least a half dozen slipgizzle owls that Ambala and even Tyto, your old hatching ground, have reported."

"What would an owl, or any creature from the Hoolian kingdoms, have to gain if war breaks out? If they were ruled by these mad bears from the Far Ice who worship a stupid mechanical clock, what would they gain?"

"Soren!" Otulissa said sharply, and clacked her beak in reprimand. "There is no time for wondering. We must act."

"You mean declare war, before the young bears return with the allies secure?"

"Of course not! I have a more—how should I put it?—conservative approach."

Soren blinked and cocked his head at what would have been an impossible angle for any other kind of creature. The word *conservative* and Otulissa just did not match up. "Do tell!"

"I think you and I need to go out on a reconnaissance flight. Now! In broad daylight, when supposedly owls never fly."

"Otulissa, be realistic. We are two old owls."

"Old warriors," Otulissa interjected.

"All right, old warriors. You have one eye. My talons are gnarled and arthritic. I doubt they'd even fit into battle claws."

"Yes, they will. Try this liniment. Cleve brewed it himself."

Soren's beak gaped. "You had all this planned, didn't you?"

"Not exactly."

"What do you mean, 'not exactly'? You never equivocate, Otulissa. I've known you too long and too well."

"Well, all right, yes. I think these bears of the Nunquivik, the Roguers, might be coming toward us. But the disappearance of Svern is mystifying, at least in the way Svenna described it. There is something else coming, and it might be beyond our control unless we find out what it is soon." She took a step toward Soren and gently placed the small pot of liniment before him. "Listen to me, old friend. It's time for us to claw up and fly. I might be missing one eye; you might have creaky bones." *They don't even feel hollow*, Soren thought, for suddenly he felt heavy. Heavy and so old. "But we can do this!"

She stretched out a single talon and touched him. He clamped his eyes shut for a moment. "What will Cleve think?" Soren asked.

"Cleve hates war. He's a gizzard resister. You know that as well as I do. What would Pelli have thought?"

"Oh, Pelli," he sighed as he thought of his old mate, who had died the summer before. "She would have said go—go for the children's sake."

"So?" Otulissa opened wide her huge dark eyes. He could see his own white face reflected in them.

"We fly now." He reached for the liniment.

The two owls, one a spotted and one a barn owl, flew out of a secret exit of the tree, almost directly into a fog bank that had enveloped the island of Hoole, which seemed a blessing. Their flight would be concealed for at least a while.

"You all right, Otulissa, with your single eye?"

"Don't fret, Soren. I see more with my one eye than most owls see with two. Don't underestimate old owls. I've still got my brain. I've still got my plummels. I can tell a maverick wind coming before it even decides to go maverick."

Soren himself tipped his plummels, those delicate fringe feathers that not only soften the sound of their flight but also detect the most minute wind shift. From the streaming wet winds, Soren sensed that they were approaching the Ice Narrows.

"Maximum climb," he commanded. But none of his commands were delivered aloud. So they flew close and used a code-signaling system with their wing tips and tail feathers. Even in the thick fog, they did not want the puffins to know they were anywhere near and launch into their insanely stupid chatter. When they had cleared the Narrows and were bearing north by northeast, heading between Elsemere Island and the Ice Dagger toward the Hrath'ghar glacier, the fog began to lift. They flew on past the glacier to the far edges of the Hrathlands.

As Soren looked on, he realized that the last earthquake had rearranged quite a bit of this landscape. The N'yrthgar Straits, frozen solid now, seemed closer the Nunqua Sea. It was not merely a question of a rejiggering of the land but actually the surface; the texture of the land seemed to have changed. From an owl's-eye view, this change was clear.

"How odd!" Soren whispered, then signaled that he was going down to investigate but that Otulissa should keep a look-out from above. The barn owl went into a steep dive. He landed on top of one of the runnels and began walking tentatively along it, peering at these odd swellings. *These are . . . oh, what's the old Krakish word? Mydlsvarls!* And in that same moment, the ice seemed to split open and swallow Soren.

Otulissa emitted a panic hoot and staggered in flight. Soren was gone! She felt herself going yeep. The split in the ice gaped at her from below as if to suck her in. She was spinning down-ward, having lost control of her flight. An immense clawed paw reached out of the crack. "NO!" she screamed, and began to pump her wings and clamber her way up and out from her own spiral toward death. She only had one thought in her mind. *Back . . . back to the tree. This is war!*

CHAPTER 31

The Namara

The cubs headed now due north and east from the Slough toward the MacNamara territory. Their mood was somber, and each bear held the vivid image of the beautiful, slain wolf Alasdair in their memory. They were anxious and yet they were driven by her final words: *Go to the Namara.*

Jytte slowed just a bit and looked up. The night had melted into the dawn. The star ladder with the blue mist had dissolved into the new gray of the morning. And the world, in Jytte's mind, seemed a little bit emptier.

"I miss her too," Stellan said, plucking the thought right out of his sister's mind.

"I think we're on track," Froya said even though the stars were gone. The MacNamara clan's territory had been the least disturbed by the earthquake. "We should be approaching Broken

Talon Point in a few hours. And this head wind is shifting. We'll make better time as it comes 'round to the south."

It was less than an hour when they spied a wolf approaching them.

"A scout!" Jytte said.

"The question is MacNamara or MacHeath?" Froya asked. "The two clans' territories are woefully close. And they are enemies."

The four bears slowed and looked suspiciously at the wolf.

"Glyncora!" the wolf announced. "MacNamara clan. You seek our chieftain?"

"Indeed." Stellan slowed to a stop and instinctively began to lower himself into a series of submission postures.

"No need. What is your mission?"

"We come from the Great Ga'Hoole Tree, sooner than we had planned, as we now have some alarming and very urgent news."

"Follow me to the gadderheal."

But soon the scout stopped at a cairn of carved bones that rose out of the snow. A fox peeked out from behind the cairn.

"Aah, Ailfryd. Keeping things tidy, I see," Glyncora said.

"Of course!"

"Foxes?" Jytte asked. They had seen so few, and this one was red, not white like the foxes of the Nunquivik.

"Yes, this is Ailfryd. She guards this sacred spot. This is where Hordweard, the first Namara, murdered her brutal mate,

MacHeath. We keep it as a monument to remind others who have been abused of Hordweard's courage."

Ailfryd dipped her head. "My honor, Glyncora."

"It has always been female red foxes who have been members of the fox guard, the *Sionnach* as it is called. The story of Hordweard has been carved in these bones. But there is not time now for us to tell that tale since your message is so urgent."

"*Auforaida!*" The red fox lofted her silky red tail into the wind.

"What did she say?" Stellan asked.

"'Farewell' in old wolf. Not spoken often these days, however."

They trekked on for another few leagues. Stellan caught up with the wolf, who kept a good pace. Undaunted by the deep snow, this gray wolf leaped over the biggest drifts as softly as a cloud scudding across the sky.

"Glyncora, I was wondering, will full submission postures be required when we arrive?" Stellan whispered to the scout.

"No, not at all. The Namara does not believe, particularly with visitors sent from the Great Tree, that submission rituals should be required. Not when urgent business is to be discussed, and most particularly anything to do with the MacHeaths. We have a long and troubled history with them."

From the moment they stepped into the gadderheal, the bears knew that they were in a very different place. There was an order to the seating as there had been in other gadderheals with the members of *raghnaid*, the high jury of any clan, seated close to the chieftain; then came the captains, top lieutenants, sublieutenants. But most astonishing was that the majority of these high officers of the clan were female!

The Namara stepped down. "Welcome to our clan and the gadderheal. I understand from our scout that you bring tidings from the noble owl Soren of the Great Tree."

Froya came forward. "Yes, Namara."

"And it concerns urgent business."

Froya inhaled deeply. She took a moment to reply. "Yes . . ."

"You hesitate. I sense you are, what . . . fearful?"

"The truth is, Namara, that the urgent business you referred to has become extremely urgent. We had planned to come here after stopping at some of the other clans but . . ." Oh, how to explain? Froya thought about how her brother was a dreamwalker and had seen somehow the death of Alasdair.

"Take your time, my dear, I can see you are quite upset."

"Yes. We came directly because of the scout Alasdair."

"Oh yes, I know Alasdair. The MacDuncan scout. A talented and especially intelligent wolf."

"I am sorry to report, madam, that Alasdair is dead."

"What?" the Namara barked. The other wolves began to stir and whisper to one another.

"We found her dying in the cave of the Sark of the Slough. As she lay dying, she had one command for us. These were her exact words: 'Quint . . . go . . . go to the Namara . . . the Namara!'"

"Quint!!!" all the wolves barked at once.

"Quiet!" the Namara ordered. There was an instant hush. She stepped closer to Froya. "Tell me, bear. Her neck was slashed, right? And then a deep tear on her chest?" Froya nodded. The Namara then turned to the rest of the wolves in the gadderheal. "She has been murdered. Murdered by a slink melf of the MacHeath clan! "

"Heya. Heya," the wolves softly snarled to one another, nodding as if in agreement with what their chieftain had just said. The Namara paused for a long time, then turned her eyes to a high-ranking she-wolf who wore the bone chain necklace of the raghnaid. They seemed to exchange a silent thought and then nod.

"Our suspicions are confirmed," the Namara said softly. "But tell us more about your talks with the other wolves and owls you have been sent to on this mission."

Briefly, Stellan summarized their successes with the MacNabs and then the owls of Ambala and Silverveil, and their setback with the MacDuncan clan. Then he told the Namara about how Third had been nabbed by the imposter bears who had dyed their fur brown. Just as Stellan was reciting this, he was suddenly aware of something stirring in his sister's head. He stopped abruptly and looked at her. "Jytte, you have something to say?"

"Just remembered something. I read it in Ezylryb's diary— the one I read for extra credit. Ezylryb said that he suspected during the War of the Ice Talons that a MacHeath might have visited the dye pots of the kraals for a camo operation."

"Camo operation?" the Namara asked.

"Yes, camouflage. I don't know why I didn't think of that at the time we were attacked and Third was snatched." Jytte opened her eyes wide. "Do you suppose that . . ."

"Heya! Heya!" The air stirred with the soft snarling of the wolves.

The Namara leaped up. *"Gloyschnyrr!"* she rasped in a deep voice.

Jytte slid her eyes toward Glyncora. "Rough beast from hell—a traitor. That's what it means," she told Jytte. "You young'uns have revealed a traitor. Lupus bless you for your studies of the papers of the great warrior Ezylryb."

"It is not simply the MacHeath clan that is traitorous," Third said suddenly. There was a flickering light in his eyes, the same light the bears sometimes saw when he emerged from a dream. But he had not been asleep, not been dreaming. "There is another gloyschnyrr." The old wolf word rolled off his tongue as if he had always spoken that ancient language.

"Another traitor?" the Namara asked.

"Indeed," Third said.

"Who might that be?" The Namara leaned forward and fixed the smallest of these bears in her gaze. She appeared to be sniffing him as well.

Third drew closer and tipped his head slightly to one side. His eyes and the Namara's seemed to lock.

"Duncan MacDuncan."

In that instant, Stellan knew that Third was right. He had not awakened from a dream, but this knowledge had suddenly come to her. Why had Stellan not been able to riddle this treacherous chieftain's mind? Perhaps he hadn't even tried. It was, after all, their first encounter with the wolves in the Beyond. They had been amply prepared to deal with owls, for they had lived and learned from them. But the wolves were different entirely. Hadn't Otulissa said they were . . . oh, what was the word she had used . . . *inscrutable!* And now Stellan realized the fear that had flooded his mind when he tried to riddle Alasdair's. She sensed that Duncan MacDuncan knew she might leave. Turn scout for another clan or become an outclanner, and that he would do anything to stop her, even murder.

The Namara began to talk crisply. "We are all poor since our return from the Distant Blue. We know that there has been trouble now for a long time between the Hoolian world, the territories that we call Before the Beyond, and these strange bears from the Far Ice, the place called Nunquivik. Duncan MacDuncan has been one of the most aggressive in reclaiming old MacDuncan territory." The Namara now turned to a silvery wolf. "First Scout Almina, did you not say that you saw Duncan MacDuncan, or you thought it was he, the during the Caribou Moon far outside his territory?"

The silver wolf stepped forword. "Yes. In the time of the Caribou Moon, I saw a wolf, similar to Duncan MacDuncan but without the usual badges and bone crests that would identify him as a chieftain, and I think he was tracking Alasdair."

"But why?" Froya asked. "Why would he be tracking his own scout?"

"Exactly!" chuffed the Namara. "But I'll answer that. For a long time, there had been rumors that Alasdair, whom many wolves called the Scout of All Scouts because of her incredible sense of smell and her extraordinary hearing, might be leaving the MacDuncan clan to become an outclanner. She was an independent-minded wolf. Duncan MacDuncan is a tightpawed wolf. What he has he wants to keep only for himself. It is my notion, mind you, it's only a notion, that he was fearful that another clan might try to claim her. This idea was intolerable to him. It would work against his plan to gain more territory. Now, I had already put a watch on the MacHeath clan because if this threat from the bears of the Far Ice came to be true, the first collaborators with the enemy would be the MacHeath clan— lawless, uncivilized, ungovernable wolves if there ever were ones. Duncan MacDuncan wanted to stop Alasdair from going clanless, but he also wanted to make a pact with these egregious, unspeakable wolves of the MacHeath clan."

At that moment, a wolf bolted into the gadderheal.

"A falcon has arrived from the Great Tree." The bears looked at one another in alarm as a peregrine falcon from the first alert emergency team swept into the gadderheal. Peregrine falcons were the fastest flyers in the bird universe.

"Two leaders of the free Hoolian world are feared captured— Svern of the Northern Kingdoms and Soren of the Great Tree." A wailing rose up in the gadderheal. Jytte and Stellan fell into each other's arms. They were stunned beyond disbelief. They felt as if the world was collapsing. They had spent so long look-ing for Svern, and now this!

"This is war!" the Namara growled deeply. "We must send a message back with the falcon that we suspect the MacDuncans along with the MacHeaths clans of collaborating with the bears of the Ice Clock!"

CHAPTER 32

The Shadow of War

Three bears, one fox who had been a bear, and two owls had figured out the grand plan of the bears of the Ice Clock. And it was a most fiendish plan that would destroy thousands upon thousands of creatures as the waters of the bungvik would be unleashed through the mechanism of the clock. It was as if Uluk Uluk, Illya, Svern and Svenna, Soren and Otulissa each held in their paws or talons a piece of a puzzle and had fitted them together into a scheme foretelling the worst catastrophe ever and the guarantee of the triumph of evil.

Otulissa now perched in the parliament with a large map and a pointer branch.

"This is where Soren disappeared, was swallowed, if you will, by a crack in the ice." She felt a shiver pass through her gizzard as she recalled the clawed paw snaking out of that crack to grab her. It was a miracle that she had escaped. She had to show herself as steady. The owls gathered in this parliament were in a state of shock. It would not do for them to pick up in any way these gizzardly quivers that racked her body.

"Is the crack still there?" asked a great gray named Elvind, a member of the ministry of war.

"No, and that is the interesting thing," Otulissa replied. "I was really so panicked on my flight back to the tree that I couldn't quite figure it out, but just in the last few minutes, it struck me. The patterns that I described from our perspective of the land when flying over were very similar to what we called in old Krakish mydlsvarls, or frost tunnels, also called gongs. This came to me when I did another flyover and saw no evidence of the crack. There is only one thing that could cause a crack like that to seal so quickly. And that's a low frost-density permeation rate."

"Huh?" said several owls.

"Don't ask me to explain it. When I was a young'un, as you know, I studied quite a bit under the tutelage of our great sage Ezylryb. One focus of my studies was the physics of frost density and evaporation rates, FDER, analysis. The perfect balance between the two forms frost tunnels. And though they are shaped differently than Yinqui listening dens with their ice conditions from the old smee holes and myldsvarls, both have excellent sound-conducting qualities."

"But are you saying these frost tunnels are natural or that these bears of the Nunquivik made the tunnels?" asked Peanut, an elf owl, also in the ministry of war. She had flown in the Frost Beak unit in the last great war.

"Absolutely not. Those bears of the Far Ice might know about clocks, but they could no more make these frost tunnels than . . . than . . ."

"Fly?" Elvind ask. There was a subdued churring from the owls. But this of course was no time for jokes.

"The realization I came to is that not only is Soren stuck in one of these frost tunnels, but these frost tunnels can and probably will direct all the water from the rumored bungvik to us! The bears of the Ice Cap did not build them, but they discovered them, and realized how helpful they could be to their master plan."

"Great Glaux," several owls muttered.

"Yes, we are in the crosshairs of possibly the greatest deluge known in our history," Otulissa said somberly. She did not add that she had read about another such deluge in the time of the Others in one of Ezylryb's volumes. It was so fantastical she hardly could believe it when she first read about it. An Other who went by the name of Noah had gathered up several animals of all species and took them off in an ark, a kind of Other's invention that floated across seas. "But here's the thing. I feel that they know that we have the key. Before they make their move to wipe us out, they want to have the key in their possession, for we could stop the clock that would then stop that torrent of water. Because of the studies that I previously mentioned, the FDER analysis, they must release the waters of the bungvik on the very edge between the Moon of the White Rain and that of the Silver Rain. Or in the bear lunar schedule the third of the Seal Moons and on the cusp of the First Cracks Moon. That will be the ideal time for the proper frost density and the phase of the moon. The pull between the moon and the sun at that time will be the strongest and cause massive flooding."

"That gives us almost two moons to stop the clock."

Otulissa nodded and at the same time seemed to wilf. In an instant, she was half her size. "And less than that to save Svern and our dear king, Soren. Within that short time, we must amass an army and invade. I want to meet with the ministry of war immediately following this gathering. Understood?"

"Yes, General!" several of the older owls replied. Otulissa glanced at her mate, Cleve, and saw that he too had wilfed. It must have been the older owls calling her general. This would be difficult for him. Cleve simply did not understand conflict, war, of any kind. He was a gizzard resister, a healer. In his mind, everything could be mended. Then she saw him lift a talon to speak.

"Yes, Cleve?"

"And I shall meet with the medics and discuss medical transports for the wounded."

What a dear old soul he was. He might be a gizzard resister, but how many wounded owls had he saved in the time of the owl wars? He had designed the ingenious air vacuums called *kroken-bots* for transporting wounded soldiers from the field. But she did doubt that these devices could manage a wounded bear.

All through the rest of this terrible day and long into the night, the owls planned, gathering in the ministry hollow and other hollows as well as in the tree. Colliers were alerted that certain kinds of coals would be needed. Buster and his son Arvid had begun forging new battle claws and helmets. A boreal owl called simply Q for Quartermaster went over the inventory lists of all weapons, both metal and the ice ones that were stored at the tree and on the Ice Dagger and other secret stashes in the Northern Kingdoms.

Little could those owls at the Great Tree pursuing their plans for war imagine that their own king and the Yinqui Svern would most likely be the very first to die when the bungvik waters were released. And that at the very moment Svern was studying his fellow captive, the barn owl, in a deep frost tunnel where they were both imprisoned. He refrained from speaking to him until the Roguer bears left. They would disappear for short periods of time, but Svern knew there was no getting out.

Svern had of course recognized the owl immediately, but he was not sure if the Roguer bears did. They were basically fairly stupid bears. All the Roguers were. They could not compare in intelligence to those at the Ice Clock. Nevertheless, they were dangerous. They basked in their brutality, their power. And although Svern recognized Soren, he dared not say his name out loud. That would be too risky if the bears knew the prize they had—the king of the Great Ga'Hoole Tree.

"You know, it could be worse," Svern said.

"Really?" Soren blinked.

"Yes, it's not a black ort." He tipped his head down. "You see this?" He lightly tapped the nubbly hardened blisters where his ears had been.

Soren gasped. "Then I know who you are!"

Svern nodded. "But let's refrain from calling each other by name. Although these bears know who I am."

"Of course," Soren said.

"Have you figured this place out?" Svern asked.

"I think I have. Frost tunnels, right? Myldsvarls."

"Yes, the last earthquake was a blessing for the bears of the Ice Clock," Svern said. He sighed. "And I'll bet we'll be their test case when they break the bungvik."

"Not necessarily," Soren replied.

"What? You see a way out of this place? No one knows where we are. We don't even know where we are, exactly."

"You don't know Otulissa," Soren said.

"Otu what . . . ?" *This is one coolheaded owl,* Svern thought.

"Otulissa, the spotted owl I was flying with. She wasn't caught."

"No, I don't know her." But Soren was not looking at Svern.

Soren paused and shoved his head close to Svern, who was sitting down. Soren's beak and Svern's muzzle were just inches apart. "But . . . um . . . what do you think of the ice here, Yinqui? You think you could reach my daughter?"

Great Ursus! Blythe. The owl was right. Why had he never thought of this? The frost tunnels were so similar to Yinqui listening dens. There was only one way to tell. He stuck out his tongue and licked the ice. His tongue didn't stick. Perfect frost dew point.

Svern began to lightly tap his code name onto the ice. Soren tipped his head first this way, then another.

"Hurry, they're coming back!"

CHAPTER 33

A Reunion

"It froze!" Jytte exclaimed as the four bears led by Glyncora stood on the very tip of Broken Talon Point that jutted out into the Sea of Hoolemere. The deep green sea that they had swum through in the time of the Copper Rain now stretched white before them. The winter moons, the moons of the White Rain, had finally come.

"Look!" Froya said. "I think I can see the island of Hoole and maybe even the Great Tree."

"With this wind and this ice, you should be there before dawn," Glyncora said. Then she lifted her muzzle. "You see that constellation there and the very bight star low on the horizon?"

"Yes," Froya replied. "The owls call that the Little Raccoon."

"Well, we call it the Caribou's Antlers. You keep two points easterly between that star and the third star in what the owls call Grank's Anvil and that will be your most direct route in this wind." She paused. "So off you go!" And the gray wolf, her pelt now silvered by the rising moon, bent down on her front knees, then lifted her tail, which blew like a bright comet in the wind, as the yosses slid down the slope of the talon and onto the ice. Stellan was the last to leave, and before he did, he reached out with his immense paw and touched the wolf's shoulder.

"Auforaida, my friend."

"Auforaida," the other three yosses cried.

The ice was slick. It was fast. When they were halfway there, they began to see the shadows of owl wings printed against the night.

They soon heard the distinctive trill of a pygmy owl.

"Rosie!" they all exclaimed.

This was followed by her staccato chatter. "Here, here!" She swooped out of the night. Her tiny wings beat a less-than-silent tattoo on the wind.

"I have instructions to rush you directly to the ministry of war hollow. Follow me. It will be a bit of a climb for you."

Within minutes, however, the yosses were winding their way through interior passages that were barely wide enough for them. When they arrived, Otulissa blinked and breathed a huge sigh of relief. She immediately beckoned Stellan and Froya with her talon to the map. There was no *welcome back, good to see you.* She plunged right in. "I know you are anxious about your father, but we must act quickly, especially if what you suspect about the MacDuncans and the MacHeaths is true. Show us where the territories are now since the earthquake."

"That's the MacDuncan territory," Stellan said. "It's a little bit farther west than before, and they are trying to claim more land. You can see it is now closer to the MacHeath clan."

"This is shocking," Otulissa said. "The oldest and most revered clan of the Beyond consorting with these most dastardly of clans."

At that moment, Blythe broke into the hollow. "A message! A message from Svern! He's alive. He's with Soren. They are in a frost tunnel of some sort—deep in it. But the ice is *yinqua*! It can conduct. There's another Yinqui, a bear to the south. So I was able to get a cross bearing with that station and triangulate the distance. Now I know the exact location."

"We have to send a message," Jytte said in a trembling voice. "We have to give them hope."

The bears with Otulissa rushed to the code hollow. Just as they crouched down near the roots, which appeared to vibrate just slightly, there was a sound at the back of the hollow.

"No one else allowed, please. This is a restricted area!" Otulissa snapped.

The air in the hollow suddenly was threaded with a scent from the distant past. Did no one else notice it? Stellan wrinkled his nose, and he sensed the agitation in his sister's mind. *It can't be*, she was thinking. *But it is!* The two bears looked at each other in disbelief. They were almost afraid to turn around.

"You would restrict a mother from her own cubs?" a familiar voice spoke out.

"Mum!" Jytte gasped.

"She's here?" Stellan's voice broke. "Here!"

"First! Second! Jytte, Stellan." Svenna swept her cubs into her arms. They were no longer simply cubs. Stellan stood taller than his mother.

"Oh my goodness," Otulissa said softly. "We forgot to tell you. Yes, your mother is here."

"Look at you! Look at both of you!" Svenna gasped. "You are all grown up." And then an immense sob shook her. "And I missed it!"

"But we're here now, Mum. We are here . . . uh . . ." Jytte hesitated.

Don't say it, Jytte, Stellan thought. *Don't say 'we'll tell you all about how we grew up without you.' That will just be too painful.*

Otulissa broke in at just the perfect moment. "You three need to be together after all this time. Please move into Ezylryb's hollow. It will accommodate all of you and maybe you can begin with stories. Stories are great menders of times lost. Perhaps the old stories that you loved to hear from your mum when you were barely yearlings."

Svenna turned to Otulissa. "We don't need stories. We just need to be together anyplace. I just need to hug my cubs." She gulped and then made a strange sound halfway between a sob and a laugh. "But they are so big I can hardly get my arms around them!"

Meanwhile, deep within the roots of the tree, Blythe began tapping the code on the roots.

℘Ψ
ƎΨ
⊥βℵ

Svern and Soren had to wait until the two Roguer bears had gone out to hunt seal for Svern to translate the message. He finally turned to Soren.

"The code reads 'Svenna safe, cubs safe. Invasion, it's coming.'" Just then the ice began to emit the familiar ticks of another message coming through. Svern raised his paw for quiet. "This is Blythe transcribing a message from Otulissa."

It was a long message, but Svern's brain worked at lightning speed. "Here is what Otulissa says: 'Fear not, dear friends. We shall fight this odious clock and these bears who worship it. We shall fight them in the air, on the ice, on the beaches with fang and talon, with grit to glory, never backing off, never surrendering to this tyranny.'"

Epilogue

That evening, Svenna and the four bears climbed high in the Great Ga'Hoole Tree to the hanging garden, which was so carefully tended by Otulissa. There were pockets of the tree where major limbs joined the trunk and collected a variety of organic matter. By careful management, Otulissa had managed to coax into bloom species of plants and flowers, lichens and mosses never before seen on the island of Hoole. It was a somewhat enchanted place where blossoms swayed in the breeze during every season of the year. They were suspended like colorful constellations from the canopy of the tree.

Now, through a cascade of winter orchids, Svenna and the four yosses looked up as the Great Bear constellation climbed into the night. She spied the skipping stars and put an arm around each of her own as if to hold them tight and not have them skip away. *How,* wondered Svenna, *can I feel such peace on this night when the world is on the brink of war?*

Stellan riddled every single word in his mum's head. He leaned in close to her ear.

"Don't worry, Mum. We are here. We have this night. We are all together."

"Ah, my riddler!" She sighed and then turned to Jytte. "And my ice gazer. Yes, tonight—we have each other."

In that same moment, a wedge formation of owls flew overhead. "The Strix Struma unit," a voice behind them whispered. It was Otulissa. "And the Frost Beaks will follow." She paused. "Glauxspeed!" she cried out.

"Glauxspeed," the bears echoed, and waved their paws.

And Jytte could not help thinking of that first night they had spent in the Great Tree, when they had looked at the same constellation of the Great Glaux and that of the Great Bear, and thought how truly they were one and the same. And how she had said to her brother, *Maybe it's all the same, Stellan. We see paws and shoulders. The owls see wings.*

"All the same," she murmured to herself. "All the same even on this night of a coming war."

About the Author

Kathryn Lasky is the author of over fifty books for children and young adults, including the Guardians of Ga'Hoole series, which has more than seven million copies in print and was turned into a major motion picture, *Legend of the Guardians: The Owls of Ga'Hoole*. Her books have received numerous awards, including a Newbery Honor, a Boston Globe–Horn Book Award, and a Washington Post–Children's Book Guild Nonfiction Award. She lives with her husband in Cambridge, Massachusetts.